᠁ ♡ ᠁

Bunwinkle turned to him, and they said at the same time, "The keys!"

"Forget the couch potatoes—we've got a bigger mystery on our hooves." Bunwinkle wiggled her body in excitement.

This was the opportunity Horace had been looking for. He could teach Bunwinkle how to be a proper pet and save Eleanor from her worries.

"It means, my dear assistant, that we are going to solve the case of the missing keys."

"*Partner.*" Bunwinkle sat down with a loud thump. "You're not better at finding clues, Horace. I figured out Andie's mysteries as fast as you."

Why must she be so difficult?

"Oh, all right." He sighed. "We'll be partners."

Also by PJ Gardner

Horace & Bunwinkle:
The Case of the Rascally Raccoon

P J GARDNER

HORACE & BUNWINKLE

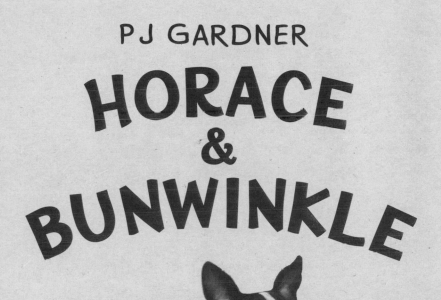

ILLUSTRATIONS BY
DAVID MOTTRAM

BALZER + BRAY
An Imprint of HarperCollinsPublishers

Balzer + Bray is an imprint of HarperCollins Publishers.

Horace & Bunwinkle
Text copyright © 2020 by PJ Gardner
Illustrations copyright © 2020 by David Mottram

ISBN 978-0-06-294655-3

Typography by Laura Mock
21 22 23 24 25   BRR   10 9 8 7 6 5 4 3 2 1
❖
First paperback edition, 2021

🦴 ♡ 🦴

To Charlie,
who came up with the names
Horace and Bunwinkle
and kindly let me use them

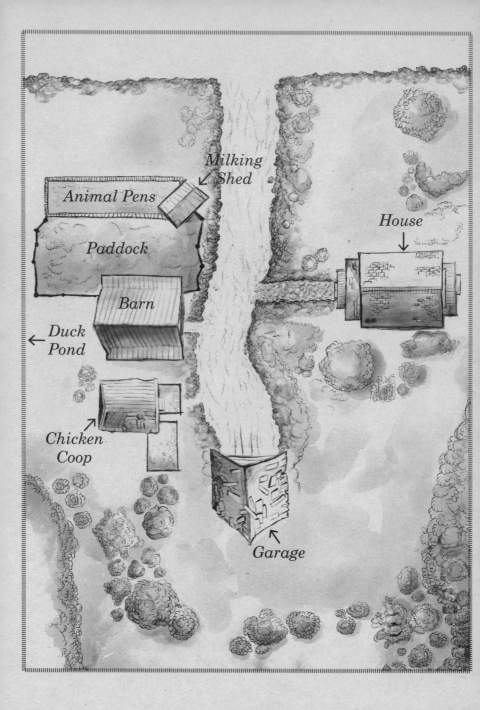

Animal Pens

Milking Shed

Paddock

House

Barn

Duck Pond

Chicken Coop

Garage

1

The Homestead

Horace Homer Higgins III was gravely ill. His head throbbed. His stomach ached. And his sniffer was clogged. This happened every time he rode in the car. Too many sights rushing by in a blur. Too many smells crowding up his nostrils. It was terribly unpleasant, and it made him oh so sick.

To make matters worse, Eleanor—that was the name of his human—had forced him to wear the Big White Cone of Shame. It was enough to make a lesser dog hang his head. But not Horace. Horace was a Boston Terrier from New England. And New Englanders were always calm, composed, and courageous—just like Horace's hero, the sixth president of the United States, John Quincy Adams.

"Are you sure he's not going to pass out?"

The voice belonged to Eleanor's friend Jennie. She was holding him in her lap while Eleanor drove. Normally, Horace loved to sit with Jennie. She always had a treat for him and smelled a bit like french fries. But today he was too upset to enjoy her.

"He's fine." Eleanor laughed. "He's just excited to get to his new house."

Horace's body shook harder, this time with irritation. He was *not* excited. He'd been quite happy in the city. He didn't want a house—he liked the little studio apartment they'd had. It was easy to guard Eleanor there; she was never out of his sight, except when she had to visit the privy. Plus he could nap and bark at the birds through the front window without ever having to get out of bed.

"He's going to love it out there." Eleanor ran a hand down his back. "Aren't you, baby boy?"

Absolutely not.

Horace swung his head toward the window, accidentally hitting Jennie in the face with the

Big White Cone of Shame.

"Can I take this thing off him?"

Eleanor sighed. "Okay, but you'll have to watch him. I didn't put any ointment on his legs before we left."

Jennie freed him from the detestable device and tossed it onto the back seat.

Oh, sweet relief. Now he could lie down in comfort. Horace pawed at Jennie's legs, searching for a suitable place to situate his body, then turned around three times to make sure the spot was nice and soft. Once he had everything to his liking, he snuggled down until his sniffer rested on her knees, where the smell of french fries was strongest.

"Why does he need the cone anyway?" Jennie asked.

Eleanor glanced at him, her brown eyes filled

with worry. Then she whispered, "O.L.D."

"What?"

"Obsessive licking disorder—O.L.D. His last vet, Dr. Mallard, told me Horace has the worst case of it he's ever seen."

Horace sniffed. Dr. Mallard didn't know the first thing about dogs. He was always telling Eleanor to take Horace for a walk and to not feed him cheese. And he absolutely insisted that licking was wrong. What a quack! That was what dogs did; that's how they got clean. And it was important to be clean. Cleanliness was next to dogliness.

Jennie nodded, then yawned so wide Horace could see all her teeth. "Remind me again, why did we have to leave so early?"

"I need to get out to my animals. My old friend Clary Hogland took care of them yesterday, but I don't want to impose on her again."

Animals? Horace's ears perked up. That didn't sound good.

"So you're really going to milk goats and shear alpacas, huh?" Jennie grinned at her friend.

"Yes, ma'am, I am," Eleanor said.

Goats? Alpacas? Horace shuddered. Where on earth was Eleanor taking him?

A farm. That's where she was taking him.

He smelled it long before they turned off onto a gravel road and he saw horses in fields, before the pasture full of cows and stacks of hay overworked his sniffer and made his eyes water.

Eleanor pulled into a gravel driveway and brought the car to a stop.

His mouth fell open.

"I'm calling it the Homestead," she said. "What do you think?"

"I think you've lost your mind." Jennie laughed.

Horace had to agree. The Homestead wasn't much to look at—a barn, a run-down house, a few animal pens, and a chicken coop at the far end of the property. And dirt *everywhere*. He'd never be able to keep his fur shiny and clean here.

And how on earth was he going to protect Eleanor? It was wide open. Anything could wander in at any time.

It was truly the most depressing thing he'd ever seen. If he'd been a lesser dog, he would have cried.

"The moving van will be here soon. Let's unload the car," Eleanor said, pulling her curly brown hair into a ponytail.

The disgusting odors grew stronger when the car door opened. Horace gagged. His poor sniffer couldn't take much more of this. He closed his eyes and buried his nose in Jennie's leg.

"Sorry, big guy, I've got to unload."

Horace crawled off her lap, curled up on the seat, and covered his nose with his paws. This was the worst day of his life.

Jennie leaned close and whispered, "It's going to be okay, I promise. Even if she did drag you out to the boonies." Then she disappeared to help with the boxes.

He sighed heavily and began licking his legs. A few minutes later, Eleanor scooped him up from the seat. "No more of that, Horace, or you'll have to wear the cone."

Hmph.

"Oh, don't pout." She kissed the side of his face. "Be a good boy and come see your new home." She set him down on the front porch. "You're going to love it even more than our old place. I promise."

Despite his misgivings, he followed her into the house. Jennie stood in the middle of the family room, a confused expression on her face.

"Did it always look like this?"

Eleanor smiled. "No, I fixed it up."

"I knew Mrs. B shouldn't have let you read all those Little House books."

"What? It looks cheerful."

"Cheerful" wasn't the word Horace would've used. In fact, cheerful wasn't anywhere on the list of words he would have used. Dreadful, *that's* the word Horace would have used. Everything was made of wood—floor, ceiling, walls, everything. And it was decorated with that material that irritated his sniffer—burlap.

Jennie poked her head into the kitchen, then turned to look at them. "Did you buy a butter churn?"

Eleanor glanced at her watch. "Oh, look, it's

time to check on the horses. Come on, Horace, I'll introduce you."

No, thank you.

Horace wasn't interested in meeting the horses, or any of the animals for that matter, but before he could hide, Eleanor picked him up and carried him out of the house.

The horses lived in the barn, which was directly across the gravel drive from the house. To its right, a chain-link fence surrounded pens for the alpacas and goats, and to its left was the chicken coop.

Eleanor hummed a happy tune as she went.

How could she be so cheerful?

"Oops, gotta feed these girls while I'm thinking about it." Eleanor set him down on what felt like a field of jagged rocks. When he tried to follow her into the coop, she blocked his way.

"Sorry, baby boy, I know how you feel about birds, and I don't want you trying to chase these away."

Horace detested birds. The unnatural way

they moved, flapping their wings up and down. It was impossible to predict their flight patterns, which meant it was impossible to protect Eleanor from them.

And then there were the feathers. He shuddered. Hideous.

But there weren't any birds in the coop. Horace saw a large nesting box in the back, an area to walk around, and a roof to keep out the sun and rain. But no chickens. According to the hand-painted sign on the door, there should be at least six.

WELCOME TO CLUCKINGHAM PALACE!

RESIDENTS:

Chicka Dee

Shell E. Winters

Sonja Henney

Eggness Gray

Annie Yolkely

and Gladys

"Hey, girls!" Eleanor called out, tossing feed on the ground.

A line of little yellow chicks marched out of the nest.

"Just think, in about six months we'll have all the fresh eggs we could ever want," Eleanor said with a huge grin. "Huh, Gladys? Right, Chicka Dee?"

She spoke to each of the chicks, calling them by name, but they didn't pay her much attention. They were too focused on the feed. One chick followed a trail of it until she stood across the fence from Horace. When she lifted her head, her eyes grew round.

"Wolf!" she shrieked.

The other chicks immediately panicked. They scurried around, bumping into one another and screaming, "WOLF!"

Horace sighed. Birds really were foolish creatures.

"I'm a dog, not a wolf," he explained.

"Wolf!" they cried in unison.

"No. I said I'm not a wolf. I'm a—"

"Horace, stop barking at the chicks." Eleanor walked out of the coop, frowning. "You're scaring them."

The door slammed shut behind her, sending another wave of panic through the group.

"THUNDER!" the chicks shrieked.

Hmph. Scaring them indeed.

Still shaking his head, Horace followed Eleanor into the barn, which was cool and dark and full of hay. The odors here were slightly less horrendous, and the soft dirt floor was a welcome relief for his paws. And there was music—a violin, if he wasn't mistaken.

"Did I leave the radio on?" Eleanor asked.

The music cut off suddenly.

How odd. Horace frowned.

Eleanor led him around the tall bales of hay stacked in the center of the barn. There he found the two oldest horses in creation standing in side-by-side stalls with matching innocent expressions. But it wasn't their expression or even their age that made Horace pause. It was their size. They were enormous. There would be trouble if they became aggressive. He stood in front of Eleanor, prepared to attack if one of them so much as neighed.

Unfortunately, Eleanor didn't seem worried. She walked past Horace and checked the radio. "Hmm. Weird. Anyway." She turned to rub the muzzle of the black-spotted horse. "How are you today, Smith?"

He neighed loudly, making Horace's body tense. Was the horse going to attack? Horace raced forward but stopped short when Eleanor laughed.

"That good, huh? And how about you, Jones?" She ran her other hand down the neck of the gray horse in the next stall.

He flicked his ears back and forth and rubbed his muzzle on her arm.

"Fellas, this handsome gentleman is Horace. He's going to help me take care of you." She waved him closer, but Horace was frozen in shock. Take care of them?

Finally she walked over and picked him up. "Come on, I want them to get used to you so there aren't any problems."

There wouldn't be any problems if they knew what was good for them.

"Hey! Moving guys are here!" Jennie's voice rang through the barn.

"Gotta go." Eleanor lowered Horace to the ground. "Don't leave the Homestead."

Without another word, she rushed off.

Before he could follow her, Smith, the spotted horse, bent his head low. Horace took a step back, then squared his shoulders and faced the creatures. He would be brave—just like that great New Englander Ethan Allen, when he attacked Fort Ticonderoga in the Revolutionary War with fewer than a hundred men.

"So you're a florist, eh? Can't see how. Got no thumbs."

A florist? Horace tilted his head. What on

earth was the spotted horse talking about?

The gray horse gave Horace an apologetic look. "You'll have to forgive my brother. His hearing's not what it used to be, and he gets a bit confused." Then the horse turned and yelled. "His name is HORACE!"

The first horse nodded, then buried his muzzle in the feed bag in front of him. Jones leaned closer. Horace backed up a few steps. Better to be safe.

"Sure is nice to meet you, young fella."

What a polite animal. Maybe the horses didn't pose a threat after all. True, the brother was strange, but he seemed harmless. In fact, they both did.

"Yes, sir, nice to get some new animals in the neighborhood, what with someone rounding up critters."

Horace tilted his head. "Someone is taking animals?"

The old gray horse nodded. "Terrible thing, sneaking in and snatching an animal from his home like that. Can't imagine what they're doing with 'em."

A pet thief? Good heavens, this place was even more dangerous than he'd realized. They needed to go back to the old apartment, where it was safe.

"But who's taking them?"

"Ghosts," Jones said.

So the horses were harmless but deranged, Horace thought. Perhaps *all* the animals on the Homestead were foolish.

"Yes, but you see, there's no such thing as ghosts," Horace informed the horse.

Jones squeezed his lips together and gave him a serious look. "Sure are. I seen 'em. Tops of their heads, anyway. White as snow. Heard them too. They kept whispering. Couldn't make out what they were saying, but I reckon it was spooky stuff."

"That can't be . . ." Horace stopped. Why was he arguing? Better to end the conversation and get back to the house, where he could watch over Eleanor . . . and possibly clean his fur. "Yes, well, I'll keep a lookout for them."

Jones leaned his head down again. "You be careful out there. Don't walk in any shadows. That's where they get you."

"Right. Thank you. It's been very nice speaking

16

with you. I bid you good day." He turned and casually walked around the stack of hay. As soon as he was out of sight, he raced for the barn door.

He didn't stop moving until he was inside the house. Ghosts and wolves and disappearing animals? It was utter madness here. He curled up on the floor in the kitchen and started licking his legs.

And that's where he stayed. He kept licking while the moving men unloaded furniture, while Eleanor and Jennie unpacked boxes, and while the sun set. He probably would've stayed there the whole night if a knock on the door hadn't interrupted his pity party.

"Hey, Ellie, I brought pie," a friendly voice called out.

"Clary, you didn't have to do that." Eleanor grinned at the short, round woman standing in the doorway. Two little girls wearing matching floppy hats and overalls stood next to her. Their eyes lit up when they saw Horace.

"You have a puppy?" one squealed.

"He's so cute!" the other shrieked.

Horace froze, bracing for the pinching and the

pulling that were sure to follow. But the girls were surprisingly gentle.

They held him and petted him and scrunched up his face and kissed him. They even had a treat for him—cheese. Eleanor said cheese was unhealthy for him, but he couldn't refuse it. That would have been impolite. No, better to eat every bite and spare their feelings.

"Can we get a puppy, Mama?"

"Please. Please. *Please.*"

Their mother ran a hand through her pale blond hair. "We'll see."

Eleanor smiled. "You're always welcome to come over and visit, girls. And if you come back in a week, you'll get to meet Horace's new sister."

A sister? He didn't need a sister. Besides, Eleanor had more than enough animals without adding another dog. Maybe she was just saying that to cheer up the little girls. Yes, that was probably it. She certainly didn't need another pet. She had him.

2

A New Family

Eight zoomed around her pen, squealing with excitement.

"Adoption Day! Adoption Day!"

All her brothers and sisters had already gone home with their forever families, and today was her turn. Good thing too. Without the other piglets, Eight had been bored out of her gourd. There was no one to play Name That Stench, or I Dare You to Eat That, or Bite the Tail with. And it just wasn't the same to bite your *own* tail.

Plus she didn't like being alone in the barn at night. There were spooky noises, and it got cold without someone to snuggle. Even if that someone was Eleven and he kicked you in the snout while he slept.

That was another thing. How had Eleven gotten adopted before her? He was a total jerk and not nearly as cute. He didn't have perfect black-and-white markings or blue eyes or a little pink heart right between his nose holes. It didn't make any sense.

Bub, the guy who took care of her, walked in as Eight circled her trough for the bajillionth time.

"Looks like someone's eager to meet her new family."

Bub opened the gate of her pen, and Eight took off running. She couldn't wait another second. She raced around the barn, but they weren't in there. They weren't outside the barn either.

"They aren't here yet, little one. We need to make you presentable first." Bub got the hose and added the nozzle to the end. "Time to get cleaned up."

Cleaned Up was Eight's favorite game. It was super simple too. First you wait until the ground gets muddy. Then roll around in the mud. Finally you count how many times Bub tells you to knock it off.

Eight always won. She was the Cleaned Up world champion.

She wiggled her bottom in excitement. Bub narrowed his eyes at her. "On second thought, let's try something different."

He went into the barn and came out with a metal tub, just the right size to fit a piglet. "You're getting a bath."

Baths were awesome! As long as she kept her snout out of the water. She'd learned the hard way that water up the nose holes really burned.

After her bath, Bub put her into a new pig harness. It was black with little pink hearts, and it matched her nose perfectly. She couldn't wait for her new family to see how adorable she was.

Eight parked herself next to the door of the barn and stared up the road. She waited and watched, then watched and waited. It was very boring.

She flopped down on the ground. Where were they? Something to chew on, that's what Eight needed right now. She rooted around in the hay and found a treat. It crunched like wood but it didn't taste like wood. It tasted like . . . Eleven's ears. Yuck.

Just then a big car pulled into the driveway. A woman got out, and a little pig hopped out behind her. Her family!

Eight dropped her treat and raced over.

"Hey! Hey!"

As she got closer, Eight got a better look at her new sister pig. Only it wasn't a sister and it wasn't a pig. It was a boy dog with a squashed face and a frown as big as the barn.

"You're not a pig!"

"You're not a dog!" they said at once.

Boy Dog sniffed. Then he curled his nose up. "Of course I'm not a pig. I'm a Boston Terrier, the noblest breed of dog in America."

"What's a breed?"

"It's what makes you different from others of your kind. You see how I'm black and white and I have a distinguished profile? I'm essentially the perfect example of my breed."

Eight nodded. That made sense.

"So I must be a heart-snout pig. Because that's what makes me different."

"That's not at all what I meant," Boy Dog said. "Actually, I don't have time to chat—we're here to adopt someone."

"Hey, I'm getting 'dopted today too!"

Suddenly Bub plucked Eight off the ground and held her close to his body.

Eight wiggled and squirmed. She hated being picked up. It freaked her out being so far away from the ground. Pigs were land creatures.

"Well, here she is." Bub rubbed the top of her head as he spoke.

"Oh, you're precious, aren't you? And you've got that little heart on your nose." The woman gently ran a finger over Eight's birthmark.

Eight stopped moving. The lady's touch was so soft, it tickled. It tickled a lot.

"Aaa*choo!*"

Nice Lady laughed and wiped her hand on her pants. "Sorry, I didn't mean to upset your snout."

"Like I told you on the phone, she's had all her

shots and she's been spayed, so you won't have to worry about that. She was the runt of the litter, so I don't reckon she'll get very big. But she will get bigger. And heavier."

"I figured as much. Piglets don't stay piglets forever. Right, sweet girl?" The woman ran her hand down Eight's back, then started rubbing one of her ears.

Ooo, that felt good. No one had ever done that before. Eight tilted her head to the side to enjoy it better.

Bub nodded. "You'll have to regulate her food. Pigs don't know when to stop."

Not true. Eight *knew* when to stop. She just didn't want to.

The nice lady leaned in until they were nearly snout to nose. She smelled delicious, and that trick with the ear was *awesome*. Something in the woman's big brown eyes made Eight feel all soft and warm inside too.

"What do you think, sweetness? Would you like to come home with us?"

There was a gasp from Boy Dog's direction.

Eight sighed loudly.

"I'll take that as a yes," Nice Lady said, holding out her arms.

Bub handed Eight over.

"I figured you two would hit it off. I'll go print up the paperwork. Now what should I put down for the name?"

Nice Lady lifted Eight and looked her in the eyes. Eight didn't mind being so far off the ground when her new human held her up. A moment later a big grin spread across the lady's face.

"I think it has to be Bunwinkle."

Boy Dog snorted. But the piglet formerly known as Eight grinned. She had a name. A real name.

Things went fast after that. Bub put Bunwinkle into the back seat of Nice Lady's car and rubbed his hand under her chin.

"You're going to a good home, little one, so behave."

Poor Bub. He was totally going to miss her. He had a big smile on his face, but Bunwinkle could tell he was sad. He was probably going to cry after they left. She nibbled on his hand to let him know it would be all right.

"That's enough of that," he said, pulling his hand away.

As he closed the door next to her, the other door opened. Nice Lady plopped Boy Dog on the seat.

"Why don't you ride back here, Horace. I want you to watch out for your sister pig. She's going to need your help settling in when we get home." She grinned at them. "I swear, you two could be twins."

Bunwinkle looked over at Boy Dog. "We're not twins."

He slumped down on the seat. "I know."

"'Cause you're a dog and I'm a pig."

"Correct," he said. Then he muttered under his breath, "What was Eleanor thinking? Adopting a pig."

"Hey, what's wrong with adopting a pig?" Bunwinkle asked.

"Well, you see, pigs are not pets. They're barn animals, plain and simple. Which means I am going to have another animal to watch over and no one to help me protect my human."

"I can be a protector."

"I don't think so. You're far too little."

Bunwinkle hopped up on her feet and glared at Boy Dog. "I am not!"

He looked down his muzzle at her. "Really? You really think you can follow the Guardian Creed? 'Ask not what your human can do for you—ask what you can do for your human.'"

"You made that up."

"I'll have you know John F. Kennedy said that."

"Who's that?" She glared at him. "Some dog you hang out with?"

Horace huffed. "He was *not* a dog. He was president of the United States. He came from New England, just like I do. However, if he *had* been a dog, he definitely would have been a Boston Terrier."

She tilted her head to the side and pretended to be asleep.

"Oh, never mind," he said, settling into the seat. He pawed at it, turned around three times, then plopped down with his back to Bunwinkle. As soon as they were on the road, he started licking his legs.

She watched him for a while. Long licks, over and over.

Bunwinkle shook her head. "You've got the lick-a-lots real bad."

"I most certainly do not. I'm merely cleaning myself." He gave her a snooty look.

"Whatever."

Too bad Nice Lady hadn't brought one of the other pigs with her instead of him. That reminded her. "So are the kids and the other pigs at home?"

Boy Dog stopped licking his legs and stared at her. "There are no children or creatures such as yourself at the Homestead."

"It's just you and me?" Bunwinkle's shoulders dropped.

"Not exactly."

"How's it going back there?" Nice Lady called from the front seat. "Horace, you'd better not be licking your legs."

He jumped up and put on an innocent face. Bunwinkle giggled. Boy Dog wasn't a very good liar.

"Wait, is that your name? Horace?"

"Actually, I'm a Higgins, like Eleanor. My full name is Horace Homer Higgins III."

"Horse Hoser Hiccups a Bird?" Bunwinkle frowned. "Are you sure that's a real name? It sounds kinda goofy."

Horace sat up straight and looked down his nose at her. "It's Horace Homer Higgins III, and I assure you it's a real name. Much better than yours, I must say."

"What are you talking about? Bunwinkle is a great name. It's the best. It's just long. That's all.

29

I need a nickname. Like . . . maybe . . . Winkie. Yeah, call me Winkie."

"Completely ridiculous." He sniffed. "Your name is Bunwinkle, and that is what I will call you. Just as I call Eleanor by her proper name and not Ellie or some other nonsense."

Winkie's ears perked up. "Is that Nice Lady's name? Ellie? I like it!"

Horace shook his head and turned away from her. "Hopeless."

Winkie ignored him. She put her hooves on the door handle and looked out the window. Whoa, everything was super blurry. Even blurrier than usual. She leaned her snout against the window and watched the blur until she got dizzy. Awesome!

"Want some fresh air, Bunwinkle?"

Suddenly, the window rolled down. Magic! It stopped about halfway from the bottom.

"Awww." Winkie frowned. "I wanted it to go all the way down."

She tapped the window with her snout and caught the scent of something. A bunch of somethings, actually. So she stuck her snout out the window. New smells shot up her nose holes, one right after another. She tried to count them, but there were too many.

"Wow! I can smell the whole world!"

"I wouldn't do that."

Winkie turned to see Horace staring at her with a horrified look on his face.

"You'll be sick," he said.

"Nuh-uh, I feel great."

That wasn't totally true. Her stomach did feel weird. Grumbly and rumbly. Like she needed to throw up.

And that's exactly what she did.

Winkie kept her head down while Ellie wiped off the back seat. What a mess! She'd promised Bub she'd be a good girl, but she'd already goofed up. What if Horace was right? What if she wasn't meant to be a pet?

"It's okay, baby girl." Ellie bent down and rubbed her nose across Winkie's snout. "Horace used to get carsick all the time. Didn't you, Horace?"

Horace couldn't hear her, though. As soon as

Winkie had thrown up, he'd jumped into the front seat and buried his face in Ellie's jacket.

Soon enough, they were back on the road. The windows were still open in the back, but only a little bit. Horace shoved his nose deep into the fabric, grumbling about having a sensitive sniffer. Winkie didn't know what to do, so she copied him. She stuck her snout into the car seat and found an old french fry.

"Look, Horace!"

He looked up with a frown. His expression changed when he saw what she had.

"I don't think you should eat that. Might upset your stomach. Perhaps I should hold it for you." He smacked his lips.

Winkie leaned over to give him the fry, then stopped. "You're just saying that because you want to eat it."

Horace made a *hmph* noise. "Don't blame me if you get sick again."

"I won't," she said, taking a bite of fry. Normally, she would have gobbled it up, but Horace was right. She didn't want to risk throwing up again.

* * *

"Okay, gang, we're home," Ellie announced as she pulled into the driveway of a small farm.

A warm, bubbly feeling spread through Winkie's chest. Home. She had a real home now. And she wanted to see all of it. As soon as Ellie set her down, she raced toward the barn. She knew that's what it was because it was so big.

"Wait!" Ellie called. "You're not going to stay in there, baby girl. You're in the house with Horace and me."

Winkie turned around, a huge smile on her face. Ellie really wasn't mad at her about the thing in the car! She still wanted her to be a part of the family.

"Come on." Ellie waved at her. "Come see your new home."

The house was awesome! Everything was made of wood, which meant she'd have stuff to chew on forever. And there was this scratchy material that felt great when she rubbed her head on it.

"Here's your bed." Ellie pointed to a fluffy purple thing on the floor. "Right across from Horace's."

Horace harrumphed again.

Then Ellie led them into the kitchen. "And this is your food dish."

Food!

Winkie rushed to the bowl, ready to dig in, but it was empty.

Her stomach twisted and grumbled. Bummer. After getting sick in the car, she was kinda hungry, and that french fry hadn't been enough. There was another rumble from her body, but this time it was further down. Uh-oh.

"Horace! Horace! Where do I go?" Something told her pets didn't relieve themselves in the house.

He frowned at her. "Where do you . . ." Suddenly his eyes got big. "Whatever you do, don't do it in here. Follow me."

He ran over to a small flap in the door and disappeared through it. Winkie did the same thing. At least she tried to. She ran at the door like Horace did, but her feet got caught on the bottom and she tripped, tearing the metal frame of the doggie door clean off. Her body rolled out of control until she crashed into a flowerpot. Before Winkie could get to her feet, she had an accident

of a different kind right there on the porch.

Oh no. Ellie would definitely be mad now. Super mad. Mad enough to decide piglets belong in barns, not houses. Or worse, send her back to Bub.

Winkie's whole body burned with embarrassment. Tears sprang up. She closed her eyes to stop them, but they spilled out anyway.

Something gently touched her head. It was probably Ellie getting ready to take her to take her to the barn. Winkie opened her eyes, to find Horace patting her with his paw.

"There, there. It's just a little . . . mishap." He cleared his throat. "Eleanor will get you cleaned up in no time."

Horace knew Cleaned Up?

A moment later Ellie rushed over with a roll of paper towels. "Oh, baby girl, you've had a rough day."

Winkie sniffled. Ellie wasn't mad. Neither was Horace. Maybe everything would be okay after all.

3

Pet—Tectives

Horace didn't care for weeping. It was so . . . undignified. He would have turned away, but Eleanor had asked him to watch over the piglet, and watch over her he would. However, the more Bunwinkle cried, the more he wanted to lick the tears away. Of course, that wasn't an option, as Bunwinkle was covered in potting soil and other unmentionable things.

Fortunately, her tears dried quickly. Except for the hiccups shaking her body every few seconds, the little pig seemed to be back to her normal self.

Well, not quite her normal self. She hadn't said a word since the incident, and she wouldn't meet his eyes either.

"I'm sorry I broke your door thingy. I'll be care-fuler next time." She sniffed. "If Ellie even lets me stay in the house."

His chest felt tight all of a sudden. "Of course she will. Pets always stay in the house."

Bunwinkle hopped up, a huge smile on her face. "You really think so? You're so nice, Horace! I'm glad you're my brother."

He cleared his throat. "Let's not get carried away."

She wasn't terrible. Not really. She was simply young and inexperienced. He watched her bounce down the stairs, nearly missing the last one and crashing again. Perhaps with training she could become a decent pet, perhaps even a guard pig. She simply needed a wise and dignified individ-ual, who knew the importance of proper grooming and decorum, to guide her.

Eleanor took the paper towels and such to the trash and returned with the hose.

"Okay, time to get you cleaned up."

"Come on, Horace, we're going to play Cleaned Up!" Bunwinkle bounced up and down, squealing, until Eleanor turned the hose on her. She giggled as she repeatedly fell to the ground.

Horace watched the little pig with wonder. A moment ago she'd been sobbing, and now she was as happy as could be.

"You know, a pet would never get so dirt—"

"What's the matter, baby boy, feeling left out?" Eleanor laughed and aimed the hose at him.

Horace scrambled to the far end of the porch. Rolling around in the mud was a dreadful idea. His sniffer would get clogged and then he'd be unable to detect any predators. Completely unsafe. Besides, Boston Terriers were not mudders. They did not enjoy filth.

"Oh, don't be so stuffy," Eleanor called after him.

He was not stuffy. He was on guard.

Eleanor aimed the hose at him again, leaving him no choice but to return to the house. Training would have to wait until Eleanor and the piglet were through being silly, and they would just have to protect themselves.

He snuggled into the blankets of his napping spot on the couch and inspected his legs for mud. He didn't find any, but it would probably be wise to clean his legs anyway. He was on lick number eighty-seven when a cold, wet snout touched his forehead.

"Found you!" Bunwinkle giggled and then scrambled onto the couch. She pressed her damp body against his. "Ooo, you're warm."

Here was a teaching moment. "You know, Bunwinkle, it's impolite for a pet to—"

"Look at you two, all cuddled up together." Eleanor grinned and pulled out her phone. "I have to get a picture of this."

Horace scowled. At this rate he would never be able to train Bunwinkle.

The photo shoot was interrupted by a loud crash from outside. Horace's ears shot up, and Bunwinkle hopped to her feet.

The smile fell from Eleanor's face. "That didn't sound good." She grabbed her jacket. "You two stay put. I don't want to have you underfoot while I'm dealing with whatever this is. Here." She picked up the television remote. "Why don't you watch something?"

With a troubled heart, Horace watched her walk out the back door. He should be protecting her. But if he followed, so would the piglet, and she'd definitely get in Eleanor's way.

Suddenly Bunwinkle gasped, "Food!" She jumped down from the couch and raced toward the entertainment center. She stood on her hind legs and pressed her snout against the television.

"I wish we could taste it."

Horace quickly changed the channel before she could lick the screen.

"Look!"

A cartoon dog raced across the TV screen, his markings a perfect match to Horace's. He was followed by a black-and-white pig. She and Bunwinkle could be twins; all she needed was a little heart on her snout.

"Suey, Spot," a young girl with glasses called to the animals. "Someone stole the statue of Athena. We've got to find it before they can destroy it!"

The dog and the pig touched paw to hoof and shouted, "Pet-tectives investigate!"

"What is it?" Bunwinkle asked in an awed whisper.

Horace watched as Spot jumped into the top hatch of a submarine.

"I don't know," he replied, dropping down on the floor next to her. "But I intend to find out."

They spent the whole day watching the show, which they quickly discovered was called *Andie's Adventures*. They couldn't get enough of Spot solving riddles and Suey defeating bad guys with her hooves of steel. Horace and Bunwinkle always knew where to find the clues and who was guilty. After a few episodes, it turned into a competition to see who could figure it out first. By the end of the day they were joining in each time the animated characters called out their catchphrase, "Pet-tectives investigate!"

It was, without a doubt, the greatest show Horace had ever seen. His favorite part was the way Spot cleaned his fur to give himself time to come up with a brilliant plan or to trick the villain into underestimating him, and no one said anything about O.L.D.

They had a lot in common, Horace thought. They were both handsome and smart, they both liked order and tidiness, and they both lived with a rambunctious pig with a tendency to make messes. Yes indeed, they were practically the

same dog. Maybe if Horace traveled the world, he could be a detective righting wrongs and keeping things orderly. He drifted off to sleep imagining himself at the Tower of London, searching for the crown jewels.

* * *

Horace and Bunwinkle woke up the next morning, still in front of the TV, ready to solve more
mysteries, but Eleanor wouldn't let them.

"It's a beautiful day. You should be outside."
She scooted them out the back door.

Horace immediately covered his sniffer. "Good
heavens, it smells even worse than usual."

Bunwinkle inhaled deeply. "Smells good to
me."

Horace shook his head and tried to sneak into
the house.

"Oh no you don't." Eleanor blocked the way.
"You stay out here. I don't want you turning into
couch potatoes."

Bunwinkle paused on the porch to stretch. "I
didn't see any potatoes in the couch, did you?"

"No," Horace answered, scratching behind
his ear. "Eleanor must have hidden them so we
wouldn't spoil our breakfast."

"That's too bad." She sighed. "I could really go
for some food right now."

He snorted. "I could really go for some food
right now" was Bunwinkle's favorite sentence.

44

She must have said it a hundred times in the last day. He was about to answer when she suddenly started tapping her front hooves. "Horace! Let's find them. Let's find the couch potatoes. We'd be pet-tectives, just like Suey and Spot."

Horace sat up straight. Pet-tectives. He liked the sound of that. Perhaps he didn't need to travel to be a detective. He could start where he was. The Homestead definitely needed someone with a cool head to solve problems and enforce law and order, which in turn would make it easier to protect Eleanor.

"Very we—" He was interrupted by a distant quack. Were there ducks in the pond behind the barn again? Since he'd arrived, he'd warned them repeatedly to stay away. That was his pond, and they'd better not be polluting it with their horrible feathers. Why, those—

"Horace?" Bunwinkle waved a hoof in front of his face.

"Uh, hmm." He cleared his throat. "Very well. You may be my assistant."

"No way! We're partners, like Suey and Spot. Besides, it was my idea."

He sat up straight and held his head high. "Yes, but I'm older and much wiser than you. Therefore, I should be the detective."

She rolled her eyes. "Older and grumpier, you mean."

"Idiots!" a raspy voice called out.

They both turned to see who'd spoken, but no one was there.

"You two are so dumb, it hurts."

The voice was coming from under the porch. Horace glanced at Bunwinkle and jerked his head toward the stairs.

"What's the matter?" She gave him a funny look. "Is your neck bugging you?"

It was Horace's turn to roll his eyes.

"Ha! You really are a numbskull. He's trying to tell you to look for me."

A dark gray cat emerged from under the porch, a nasty grin on her face—Smokey. Horace had heard about her from one of the goats. She was a stray with a habit of starting fights.

He turned to tell Bunwinkle it was time to leave, but the piglet wasn't next to him anymore. She was halfway down the stairs.

Horace shook his head. "Hey, isn't that Elea-nor calling us? We should probably go back to the house now."

"I didn't hear anything," Bunwinkle said.

Honestly, she had no sense of self-preservation. Couldn't she sense she was heading into danger? He had no choice but to follow. He couldn't leave her alone with Smokey.

"Why don't we go look for those couch pota-toes?" Horace tried again.

Smokey gave a dry, rattling laugh. "Those aren't real. It's just a saying humans have."

Bunwinkle stamped her hoof. "They are too real."

"Right. Like bigfoot is real." Smokey sneered. "Are you like that dim-witted horse? You think monsters roam the neighborhood eating couch potatoes and stealing animals from their homes?"

The cat sauntered away without waiting for an answer.

"What an unpleasant creature," Horace said, loud enough for her to hear.

"Yeah, and a liar. Saying couch potatoes aren't real. And what was she even talking about with that whole stealing-animals thing?"

Horace shook his head. "I'm not sure, but animals aren't the only things missing, apparently. Look." He gestured with his paw at the mess in the yard. The fencing around the goat and alpaca pens had collapsed. Most of it was in a heap near the road for garbage pickup.

Bunwinkle gaped at the mess. "So that's what that loud crash was yesterday."

"No wonder Eleanor let us watch TV the whole day. She had to clean it up and move the animals into the barn."

As they stood there, the back screen door opened, then slammed shut, and Eleanor stomped down the steps, talking into her cell phone.

"Clary, I don't know what to do." Her voice was higher than usual. "I can't find my keys anywhere, and I have to be at the bank in an hour to sign those papers or the deal won't go through. Right, I'll check there now." She rushed off to the barn.

Bunwinkle turned to him, and they said at the same time, "The keys!"

"Forget the couch potatoes—we've got a bigger

mystery on our hooves." Bunwinkle wiggled her body in excitement.

This was the opportunity Horace had been looking for. He could teach Bunwinkle how to be a proper pet and save Eleanor from her worries.

"It means, my dear assistant, that we are going to solve the case of the missing keys."

"*Partner.*" Bunwinkle sat down with a loud thump. "You're not better at finding clues, Horace. I figured out Andie's mysteries as fast as you."

Why must she be so difficult?

"Oh, all right." He sighed. "We'll be partners."

From the other side of the barn, a round of quacking filled the air. Horace whipped his head around. Those wretched ducks *had* returned to the pond.

"Where are you going?" the piglet asked him as he walked past her.

"To rid the Homestead of ducks," he replied over his shoulder.

"Uh-uh!" Bunwinkle ran in front of him and blocked his way. "If you go to the pond, you'll spend the whole day there. Who cares about ducks when we've got a mystery to solve?"

"I do." He continued around her.

"Fine." Bunwinkle wrinkled her snout. "Then I'll just investigate on my own."

Horace stopped, torn between protecting his domain from feathered menaces and protecting the case from Bunwinkle's tendency to chew first and ask questions later. She was sure to mess up the evidence.

The mystery won out.

"Very well, then." He turned up his nose with a sniff. "But after we've found the keys, I insist on clearing the pond. Otherwise the ducks will feel they have a claim to it."

"What is it with you and ducks?"

"I'm glad you asked. Du—"

"You know what? Never mind. Let's go check the couch." She trotted away without waiting for Horace's lecture on the awfulness of birds.

Bunwinkle stopped at the door. "Wait. Before we start, we have to do the catchphrase." She put out her hoof.

"Yes, good thinking. We want to do things properly." He tapped his paw against her hoof, and together they said, "Pet-tectives investigate!"

A thrill went through his body, and she gig-gled.

"Let's go find those keys," he said.

* * *

Unfortunately, the keys weren't in the couch. Horace and Bunwinkle pulled off all the cushions to be sure. They found a few pieces of candy—which the piglet ate before he could stop her—plus a great number of pens, and a dish towel, but no keys.

Nor were the keys on the kitchen counter. According to Bunwinkle, anyway. Since they weren't tall enough on their own to see up there and neither of them could jump high enough, they'd come up with a new plan—one that involved Bunwinkle crawling on Horace's back and standing there for what seemed like hours. She was heavier than she looked.

"Where do you think they could be, Horace?" she asked as her back hooves gave out and she thumped down on top of him.

"Oof." His knees buckled, and they crashed to the floor.

Bunwinkle scrambled to her hooves, an excited expression on her face. "I know. The barn. It's totally obvious."

Horace stood and stretched his back. "She's probably already looked in the barn. That's where she was heading earlier."

"Yes, but we can talk to the other animals and she can't. I bet we could get some clues from them."

She brought up an excellent point. "All right. Let's go to the barn."

On their way they passed Eleanor sitting in the car and mumbling to herself.

Fortunately, the barn door was open wide enough for them to slip through. Horace's eyes immediately began to water, and his sniffer quit working. Eleanor had moved all the animals except the chicks to indoor pens because of the fence issue, and the smell of all those bodies was overpowering.

"Oh, wow. This place is awesome. It smells like dung."

Horace shuddered.

"Now listen," he said, "before we go any further, I think we should get organized."

"Let's start with them." She pointed her snout at the alpacas.

"Sadly, they don't speak English," Horace said.

Bunwinkle shrugged. "Well, I bet the horses will know."

"Before we meet them, there's something I should tell you. The horses are quite large, so it would be wise to stay back from the stalls. Wouldn't want to get stepped on, right?" He cleared his throat. "And they're also a bit . . . odd. Well, Smith isn't odd so much as he is hard of hearing. But Jones . . . well, it might be tricky to get good information out of him."

"Horace! Horace, is that you?" Jones called out.

"Don't worry." Bunwinkle grinned at Horace. "It'll be fine. Everybody loves me."

Naturally, it wasn't fine.

When Horace introduced her, Smith snorted loudly, then turned to Jones and neighed, "Huh. Coulda sworn he called the piglet Fun Finkle. Ridiculous name for a pig, in my opinion."

"No, her name is Bunwinkle," Horace corrected him loudly.

"Huh?"

"BUNWINKLE!" he shouted.

"Butt wrinkle? Huh, can't say as I think that's much better."

Horace groaned. Talking to the horses was a huge mistake.

Bunwinkle moved closer to the stalls. "THAT'S NOT MY NAME! I'M WINKIE!"

Jones leaned down and studied her. "Winkie? Did you say Winkie?" he asked Horace.

"Er . . . yes?" Horace braced for the weirdness that was sure to come.

"You do know what a Winkie really is, don't you?"

"A pig," Bunwinkle answered. "I'm a pig."

"Oh no, it only *looks* like a pig," Jones said, backing away. "Winkies are actually evil sprites who can shape-shift to look like common farm animals. They sneak in and enchant the real animals, then lead them away to die painful, horrible deaths."

Horace sighed. They were never going to find the keys this way. "Yes, thank you, Jones. I think it's time for us to go now. Come on, Bunwinkle." He nudged her, but she didn't move.

"I . . . I wouldn't hurt anyone," she cried.

The sound of her small, shaky voice stopped Horace. "Oh no. Not the crying."

He leaned close to her face, ready to lick away any tears, but she put her head down so he couldn't see her eyes. He sighed to himself. He didn't know what to make of Bunwinkle sometimes. One minute she raced off without a care, and the next she cried because her feelings were hurt.

"And I'd never 'chant nobody." She wiped her eyes and sniffed. "I don't even know what that is."

She looked so sad and pathetic, he couldn't do anything but comfort her.

"There, there. No need for tears." he said kindly. "I mean, did William Dawes cry when he fell off his horse? Of course not."

"Who's that?" Bunwinkle hiccupped.

"He rode the same night as Paul Revere to let people know the British were coming. Just one of the many brave New Englanders during the Revolutionary War. You know, I'm from New Engl—"

A loud bleat distracted him. Horace glanced over his shoulder to where the sound had come from. The nanny goats. Of course! He should have thought of that earlier.

"Come on, partner. We've still got a set of missing keys to find. Maybe the nanny goats can help us."

Bunwinkle sniffed again, then nodded. "Okay."

The nannies weren't the friendliest animals on the Homestead. In fact, they could be downright rude. Except for Minnie—she had wonderful manners. As Horace and Bunwinkle neared the fence, one of the nanny goats whispered in the long brown ear of her friend, a nasty gleam in her eye.

Maybe this wasn't a good idea either.

Horace decided to try a little flattery. "Ladies, it's lovely to see you today."

"Ladies, it's lovely to see you today," the nanny closest to the fence mimicked in a high voice.

"Hey! That's not nice," Bunwinkle snapped.

"*Thpbt. Thpbt. Thpbt.*" The other nanny blew raspberries at them.

Horace stepped close to the fence. "Stop that!"

"Stop that!"

"Thpbt. Thpbt. Thpbt."

"Thaaat's enough!" This came from Minnie. She moved out of the shadows. "You two aaare a disgrace."

The nasty nannies made faces at her as they walked away.

"They're just lucky I wasn't in there with them. I would've bitten their legs," Bunwinkle muttered.

Horace smiled. The old Bunwinkle was back.

Minnie stared at them through the fence. "Whaaat can I dooo for you?"

"We're trying to help Eleanor find her keys. You haven't seen them by any chance, have you?"

"Eleanooor's the one who miiilks us?"

They nodded at the same time.

"Goooood woman. Alwaaays warms her haaands before milking." She nodded to herself. "Veeery thoughtful."

"She's the best!" Bunwinkle agreed.

"I saaaw her with the keeeys. Took them with her out into the coooop."

"The coop!" Bunwinkle jumped up and down.

"They have to be out with the chickens. Thank you!" she called over her shoulder.

"Thank you, Minnie," said Horace.

When he arrived, the little pig had her snout pressed to the chicken wire as she stared into the coop.

"I don't see them from here. We need to get inside and dig around, but the gate won't open." She turned her head toward him. He snorted. The wire had left an impression on her nose.

"What?"

"Nothing." He looked up so he wouldn't stare at it.

And there they were.

The keys were resting on the corner of the WELCOME TO CLUCKINGHAM PALACE! sign.

"Bunwinkle, look!"

Horace raised his chin and took a deep, satisfied breath. They'd found them. Of course, he'd done most of the work, but the piglet had helped . . . a bit.

"Yay! Now all we gotta do is knock them off that thing and take them to Ellie. And I know just how to do that." She backed up, put her head down, and charged at the fence.

Why wouldn't she listen to him? She was bound to hurt herself.

Bunwinkle hit it and bounced back. She shook her head, then backed up again. "I know why it didn't work. I didn't do the thing." Bunwinkle reared back on her hind legs and shouted, "HOOVES OF STEEL!"

"No, we don't need hooves of steel." Horace snorted impatiently. "We need to get Eleanor's attention. She can get them off the sign herself."

But Bunwinkle wasn't listening. He moved in front of her. "Will you sto—" Unfortunately, with her head down, she hadn't seen him move, which meant that instead of hitting the fence, she hit Horace.

He flew back into the fence. Stinging pain shot up his back, and he yelped. At the same time, the sign on the fence came loose and fell on Bunwinkle's head. She squealed shrilly, and six little chicks scurried out of their hutch.

"Wolf! Wolf!" they screamed. And then the smallest one, Gladys, noticed Bunwinkle. She skidded to a halt, tilted her head back, and hollered as loud as she could, "Rhinoceros!"

There was a brief moment of silence before five other chicks shrieked, "Rhinoceros!" and made a mad dash for the safety of their hutch.

"What is going on over here?" Eleanor's voice startled them all.

Horace had never been so grateful to see his human.

4

Dr. Schott

Winkie didn't know what to do. Horace was mad at her. Really mad. He wouldn't talk to her or even look at her. He sat in his seat, a bandage wrapped around his middle, licking his legs. Ellie had taken one look at their injuries and called the vet. That's where they were headed now.

She couldn't blame Horace for being upset. He'd gotten hurt because of her. And he'd gotten in trouble with Ellie. She'd been lecturing them since she started the car.

Nothing had gone right today. Mean cats. No couch potatoes. Weirdo horses who hated her. Yeah, they'd solved the mystery of the missing keys, but they'd both gotten hurt, which took all the fun out of it.

Pretty soon they pulled up to the vets' office. The sign out front read SCHOTT, SCHWINK, & SCHWANK VETERINARY CLINIC.

"Which one is our doctor?" Winkie leaned close to Horace and asked.

He frowned and scooted away from her. Winkie didn't think he was going to answer, but after a few seconds he said, "Dr. Schott."

"The vet's name is Dr. *Shot*?"

Horace nodded.

"No way. Does he . . . does he . . . ?"

"Give lots of shots?" Horace nodded again. "No one ever gets out of his exam room without at least one. Sometimes as many as four. And he gives them himself. Most vets let their assistants do it, but not Dr. Schott." He shivered. "Dreadful man."

Winkie sank down into her seat. This day just kept getting worse and worse.

Ellie put Winkie on her leash, but she carried Horace into the building.

Horace seemed calmer now. He was doing that stiff-upper-lip thing he claimed was a part of his New England heritage. Winkie tried to match him, but it didn't work. Maybe stiff lips weren't in her heart-nosed piglet genes.

The reception area made her feel a little better. There were chairs for the humans and a little play area with toys for the pets.

"Oh my gosh! Look at these two cuties! They could be twins." A pretty, young tech set down a box of cookies and rushed around the counter to kneel in front of Winkie. She practically squealed when she saw Winkie's birthmark. "Look at that little heart." Then she reached out and booped it.

Another human who found her adorable. It was going to be difficult for the lady when she found out Winkie already had a home.

Horace got the lovey-dovey treatment next. The nurse made kissy faces at him and asked, "What are you doing here today?"

"Well, this one"—Ellie nodded at Horace— "may need stitches. And this one"—she pointed to Winkie—"may have a concussion."

"Horace, what's a combustion?"

He didn't answer. He was too busy licking his legs again.

"Oh, poor babies. We'll get them in to see Dr. Schott as soon as we can."

They went and sat in the waiting area. Winkie wanted to play with the toys, but Ellie wouldn't let her. "I need you to sit here and behave, little one, while I call the bank real quick."

Bummer. Winkie really could go for something to chew. She spotted a rubber ball under Ellie's chair.

Horace sat completely still, his eyes focused on a wall covered in flyers. He didn't say anything when she talked to him. He must be so scared—he wasn't even licking his legs now. Winkie's tummy flip-flopped, and she chewed harder on the ball until it popped and Ellie snatched the pieces away from her. There was nothing left to do but stare at the wall of flyers like Horace.

Hmm, maybe she should practice her reading. Horace said all pets had to know how to read so they wouldn't get into stuff that was bad for them. She'd been watching a show that taught her letters and words. Now was the time to try it out.

There were three ads for something called beehive school, two for pet haircuts, and . . . nine missing-animal posters. They were mostly house pets, like dogs and cats, but there was a lost chicken too.

Nine missing animals seemed like a lot. Hmmm. Something tickled her memory.

"Horace, do you remember what Smokey said? Wasn't it about someone stealing animals?"

No answer.

"Blink one time for yes and two times for no."

Nothing.

Maybe something was really wrong with Horace. Maybe he had a fever like Andie did in that one episode of *Andie's Adventures*. Winkie tried to put her lips on Horace's forehead, like Andie's mother had done, but her snout got in the way.

Oh man, Horace smelled really good—like a

mix of cheese and the blankets on the couch at home.

"Stop. That tickles," he grumbled through tight lips.

"Hey, Horace, I'm bored."

He harrumphed at her, then went back to staring at the wall. So she did too.

Winkie had practically memorized the posters by the time Kissy Face Lady called their names. She led them into a room and placed Horace and Bunwinkle side by side on the exam table.

"Okay, you two, be good," she said as she left.

The vet came in a few minutes later.

He had flaming orange hair that never moved—like a helmet—and big eyes that were always wide open. His smile was super creepy. It spread across his entire face, showing every one of his teeth. The worst part, hooves down, was his voice. It was high-pitched and unnatural, and Winkie could tell he didn't normally talk like that.

"Hi there, guys," he trilled. "What are we here for today?"

Winkie winced and glanced over at Horace. His eyes were glued to the doctor, and his body was so still, he looked like a statue.

Dr. Shot bent down and got nose to nose with Horace. "It's okay, little fella, I'm going to take care of this boo-boo, and before you know it you'll be out rustling cattle again."

Winkie rolled her eyes.

As soon as Dr. Shot touched him, Horace sprang to life. He wiggled and squirmed and even growled under his breath. Winkie moved to the far end of the table so she didn't get knocked off.

"Eleanor, can you hold him still? I can't check him out when he's like this."

Even with Ellie's help, it took forever to do the exam. And the longer it took, the more frustrated Dr. Shot got. He stopped using that little-girl voice, and the clown grin never came back.

"He doesn't need stitches."

Horace sighed with relief.

"But I'm going to give him a shot of antibiotics just to be safe."

Horace tried to escape again, but it was no use. The vet gave him the shot anyway.

"What a good boy," Dr Shot said in his little-girl voice. "Yes, you are. Yes, you are."

"Why does he talk like that?" Winkie whispered to herself.

Dr. Shot heard her squeak and seemed to think she was talking to him. He put his face right up to hers. "Oh my goodness, look at this cutie."

Winkie scooted back as far as she could without falling off the table. Normally she didn't mind humans snuggling up to her, but this guy was too much.

"We love little piggies here! Yes, we do. We even talked about making one our mascot. You'd be perfect, with your little heart."

He tapped her snout a little too hard, and she ducked her head before he could do it again.

"So why is this one here today?" he asked Ellie in a totally normal voice.

"I'm worried she might have a concussion. A sign fell on her head. It wasn't very heavy, but I don't want to take any chances."

The doctor nodded and in his human voice said, "Well, let's take a look." He washed his hands with a gel that made Winkie's nose wrinkle, then grabbed something off the wall. She twisted her head. What did he have? Was it a needle?

70

No, it was a light. And he aimed it right into her eyes.

Agh! Too bright! Winkie squeezed her eyes shut, but that didn't stop Dr. Shot. He pried open her lids and shone the light again.

"Be a good girl for Dr. Schott now, or . . ."

Or what? If she fought him, would he give her a shot? Hmm, maybe it would be better to sit still. Which was exactly what she did while he went back and forth with the light.

Right eye, left eye.

Right eye, left eye.

When he finished, she couldn't see anything but a bright spot.

"Good girl," he chirped in her ear. "Now let's check for any bumps."

He ran his hands over her head, pressing down until it hurt. The bright spot had faded by this point, and she could see his expression clearly. No more smiles. No shiny eyes. He pressed harder, and she yelped. He put his face in front of hers and said in that fake voice, "Sorry, sweetheart."

In his normal human voice he said, "She looks fine, Eleanor, but keep an eye on her. If she continues to behave oddly, bring her back in and we'll do an X-ray."

Poor Horace. He had to get a shot, but she didn't.

"You know what?" Dr. Shot opened a drawer and pulled out a syringe full of clear liquid. "Why don't we give Bunwinkle a B12 injection while you're here. It's good for overall health."

The next thing Winkie knew, she was pinned to the horrible vet's side, getting a needle in the back of the neck. It didn't hurt exactly, but it didn't feel good either.

When the doctor set her down again, Horace smirked. "I told you. No one gets out of here without a shot."

When they left, Winkie practically ran out of the building.

"Stop it!" Horace griped at her. "I can't keep up. What with my injured back and all."

She rolled her eyes but slowed down.

They were almost to the car when two little girls ran over.

"You've got a pig!" they giggled. "You've got a pig!"

A woman came running up behind them. "Linn, Nea, you know better than to run away from me in a parking lot. You could've been hit by a car."

"But Mama, she has a little pig," the freckled one answered.

The one with braids giggled again and pointed at Winkie's snout. "And she's got a heart on her nose." Without warning, the girl leaned down and rubbed her nose against Winkie's heart. "It's so soft."

The girl's breath smelled delicious. Just like peanut butter cookies.

Ellie opened the car door and lifted Horace to his seat. He stretched his neck out and whispered, "See if they have cheese."

Right. If they had any cheese, Winkie was going to eat it herself.

"What are you doing here, Clary?" Ellie asked the other woman.

"Oh, we're here to get some treats for that old

horse of ours. He's been off his feed, and I'm hoping to find something that will get him to eat."

"Poor thing."

"Honestly, it's been so busy at the farm this month. Lars and the boys installed a new misting system, and it took all six of them to get it working." Then Clary whispered to Ellie, "And now that mountain lion must be back. It made off with a bunch of meat from our smokehouse. I don't know how it got in. We keep it locked."

Suddenly Horace whimpered loudly and everyone turned to him. The girls jumped up and ran to him. "Oh, poor Horace, you look so sad and hurt. You need a treat."

The freckled girl pulled a couple of baby carrots from her pocket. Horace's ears went up and he smacked his lips. The girls broke the carrots into smaller pieces.

Yes! Winkie loved carrots!

"Wait, girls, you have to ask if it's okay first," Clary said.

The girl with the braids turned to Eleanor. "Can we, Ms. Higgins?"

"Sure thing."

"Yay!" the twins cheered as they held out their hands. "Here, Horace."

He ate the carrots up in one bite.

Winkie's nose holes flared in anger. Oh, he did that on purpose so she wouldn't get any. How selfish!

"Do you want some, piggy?" The one with the braids held out a handful.

Winkie tapped her hooves.

"Is it okay if they feed her some carrots?" their mother asked.

"Sure."

The carrots were delicious. Warm and crunchy, just the way Winkie liked them.

"What's her name?"

"Bunwinkle."

The girls giggled. "That's a silly name."

From the car Winkie heard a loud snort.

"Well, girls, we need to get going." Clary pulled a little bottle of hand gel out of her purse. "Clean your hands."

"See you later, Horace. See you later, Bunwinkle." The twins waved at them.

"Hey, Horace, what's a mountain lion?" Winkie

asked as she scrambled into the car.

"It's a very large cat." He paused and then added, "They feast on piglet sisters who get others in trouble with the vet."

Ellie would protect her, Winkie was sure of it, but it still made her shiver. Then she realized what Horace had said, and she got a big grin.

"That's the first time you called me your sister."

"Hmpf."

Horace was in a bad mood for a whole day after the visit to Dr. Shot. All he wanted to do was watch his favorite show, *Dogton Abbey*, or sleep.

"Oh, come on, Horace, I apologized like a million times already," Winkie said after an especially boring episode.

He stood up, and she tapped her front hooves real fast.

"You're awake! Great."

Horace yawned, pawed at the blankets, then lay back down. He smacked his lips a couple of times, and Winkie waited. Maybe he was going to say something. He didn't. He just went back to watching the TV.

Winkie blocked his view with her body. "Pay attention to me!"

"The way you paid attention to me when we were searching for the keys?" he snapped.

Geez, was he going to stay mad forever?

"You insisted that we be partners," Horace continued, "but a partner would have listened. Any creature with manners would have listened, but not you. You had to charge ahead without thinking. It's like John Adams said, 'Everything in life should be done with reflection.'"

"Wait, who's John Adams?"

Horace stared at her like she'd grown another ear. "John Adams was the second president of the United States and a very wise man from New England."

"What does he have to do with any of this?" Winkie snapped.

"He said to think before you act." Horace's face turned red. "But you never think. That's why I wound up getting a shot. That is also why I will not investigate with you anymore."

Oh, he made her so mad!

"Hey, I got a shot too. And it was your own fault you got hurt. If you'd let me go through with my plan, nothing bad would've happened."

He glared at her. "I don't know why I thought I could train you to be a proper guard pig. You're nothing but a barnyard animal!"

Winkie felt like she'd been hit by that big sign all over again. That was the worst thing he'd ever said to her. He didn't think she was good enough to be a pet.

"Well . . . I'd rather be a barnyard animal than a big jerk like you!" She made sure to mess up his blankets before jumping off the couch.

She stopped at the kitchen door and shouted, "And your breath smells like old garbage. I didn't say anything because *I'm* nice."

With that, she stomped out of the house, making as much noise as she could.

She stomped across the back porch. She stomped down the stairs. She stomped until her snout hit the fence. She looked up into the deep brown eyes of the alpacas, and everything came pouring out.

"You guys wanna be pet-tectives with me? Horace is a butthead and I don't want to work with him anymore."

The alpacas stared at her kindly.

"He said I was a barnyard animal. And a bad partner. But he's not so great! All he does is boss me around and watch stupid TV shows. Well, you know what? I don't need him. I can solve mysteries all by myself. Mysteries like where all those missing animals from the flyers are going, or . . ." She looked around. "Like what's in that big field across the road? Yeah."

They smiled and said something in their special language.

Winkie smiled back. "Thanks, guys, you've really helped. Talk to you later."

She marched up the gravel driveway with her head up. She stopped at the road and looked around. No cars. That meant it was safe to cross. She scurried over the road and into the field of tall switchgrass before anyone saw her.

Time to put her snout to work.

Up and down the field she sniffed. Horse. Dog. Tractor fuel. Nothing special. Shoot, no clues. Well, that was okay; at least she knew the field was safe. Then she caught a whiff of something strange. Like cat fur, only stronger. And there was something else. Something sweet and . . . maybe the stuff Ellie put on her hands after she milked the goats.

She heard things too. There was a rustling as someone or something moved through the grass near her. And whispers. Someone was out there, but the grass was so high, she couldn't tell who it was. What if it was a petnapper? She didn't want to end up on a flyer. Or . . . what if it was that mountain lion? It would eat her whole, just like Horace said.

The hairs on her back stood up. This was bad. She was all alone, in a field, with a gigantic cat that wanted to devour her. Her knees shook and her tummy ached. If only she could get home, she'd never go off by herself again. But which way should she go? Everything looked the same from down there.

She heard it again. Rustling, closer this time.

Without thinking, she took off running. Where didn't matter. She just had to get away from whoever was after her. And there was definitely someone there. She could hear them chasing her through the field.

She should never have come out here by herself. She should've stayed on the couch with Horace, even if he was a big meanie.

The footsteps were getting closer. It was only a matter of time before they caught up with her. Wait. There was a barbed-wire fence. If she could get past it, she might have a chance.

Using her last bit of energy, she raced toward the fence and shimmied underneath, careful not to scrape her back on a barb. On the other side, she ran until her legs gave out and she dropped to the ground, panting for breath.

Everything was okay. She'd made it. She was safe.

Winkie relaxed. There was nothing to worry about. Except maybe for that crinkling sound. She hopped up. Had they found her again? She sniffed the air, but the scent she picked up was different—fur and something bitter.

She followed it, making sure to be as quiet as possible. Up ahead she saw a patch of black and white fur. She let out a big breath. It was just Horace.

"You decided to get off the couch after all." She

trotted toward him.

The critter jumped up and spun around.

It dawned on Winkie that she wasn't running toward Horace about the same time that a stream of nasty-smelling liquid hit her face.

5

A Royal Obligation

Horace did not have bad breath. He chewed dental treats every day to ensure it. Imagine the impertinence of that creature, saying such a thing! Let her go pout outside. He didn't care.

He settled in and enjoyed a lovely episode of *Dogton Abbey* where Lord Crinklebottom ran out of jam for his toast.

"Hey, you two, I'm going to go muck out the horse stalls." Eleanor passed through the family room, her hair pulled back into a braid. "Don't spend the whole day lying around watching TV."

Guilt soured in Horace's stomach as he watched Eleanor leave the room. He was supposed to watch out for Bunwinkle. He was the senior pet, superior in wisdom and experience, which meant he had no excuse for being mean to her. He'd probably hurt her feelings. What if she'd become so upset, she'd started crying? And then, blinded by tears, stumbled into a ditch? She could be lying there with a broken leg.

An image of the wall of missing-animal flyers popped into his mind. Good heavens! What if something else had happened? A thief? Or worse . . . what if the mountain lion had found her? He should never have let the little pig go off alone.

Worry washed over him, and he raced out the back door. Bunwinkle was nowhere to be seen. Not in the barn either, or at the pond. Where could she be? She wouldn't have left the Homestead, would she? Horace thought of her angry expression when she'd stomped away. Yes, she would.

He ran back through the house, out to the front porch, and looked out over the field across the way. The tall grass swayed with the breeze, but there was no sign of Bunwinkle.

His heart hurt as if someone was squeezing it. Eleanor would be devastated if something

happened to Bunwinkle, and he would never forgive himself. Yes, Bunwinkle was obnoxious and had a knack for finding trouble, but he was responsible for her.

He had to look for her. But he wasn't supposed to leave the Homestead. And what if he lost his way? Then Eleanor would have to search for *two* missing pets. But if he didn't go . . .

The stress of it was too much. He dropped

down and started licking his legs.

The Schott, Schwink, & Schwank mobile veterinary van passed by while Horace stared at the field. Dr. Schwank was at the wheel, a deep frown on his face. He'd probably been up at Hogland Farm. Clary had mentioned something about a sick horse.

After the van passed by, Horace saw something through the haze of dirt kicked up by its wheels. It was an animal, crouched in the tall grass. The haze cleared a bit more.

Bunwinkle!

Horace almost wept with relief. He leaped off the porch and raced to the edge of the property. He waited for her to cross the road, but she didn't.

"Bunwinkle! What's the matter?"

She lifted her head. Enormous tears leaked from her eyes. Then the direction of the wind changed, and he understood why she was so upset. Even from across the road, the stench of skunk was enough to make him gag.

He put a paw over his sniffer and backed away. "You got sprayed by a skunk."

Bunwinkle's tears turned to big, heaving sobs. "Yyyesss."

Oh, dear.

"Hey . . . now. It's going to be . . . okay," Horace called to her. "Why don't you come over here and we'll go find Eleanor?"

At the mention of Eleanor, Bunwinkle's sobs grew louder. "She's gggonna be mmmad."

Well, he would have been angry if he had to clean her up, but Eleanor never seemed to lose her patience with the piglet.

"Don't worry about that. Just come home and let her take care of you."

The sobbing stopped, and Bunwinkle nodded. "O-kay," she hiccupped.

As she crossed the road, Horace caught sight of something. It looked like the tail of a certain dark gray cat.

They didn't have to look for Eleanor long. As they walked into the courtyard, she appeared at the barn doors as if drawn by the smell.

"Oh, Bunwinkle. Stay right there. I'll get the de-skunkifier ready."

It took four doses of Eleanor's special wash to get rid of the odor. Horace could barely stand to watch. His sniffer hurt if he got within ten feet of Bunwinkle.

"What happened?" he asked later.

"Someone was in the field. They chased after me. I only got away because of the barbed-wire fence. Scared me real bad. I was running away from them when I found that rotten stunk who sprayed me."

"Skunk."

She nodded. "Stunk."

"Never mind." Horace shook his head.

Bunwinkle yawned and snuggled down into her bed.

Horace nudged her with his nose. "Could the stalker have been the mountain lion?"

"Maybe. I did smell cat fur. But there was something else. It smelled like . . . like . . ." All of a sudden her ears shot up and her eyes widened. "It smelled like the vets' office. You don't think Dr. Shot tried to steal me, do you?"

"Why would he steal you?"

"Duh. He said they wanted a pig to be their mascot."

That was true. And the mobile veterinary van had been in the area. Dr. Schwank might have been driving, but that didn't mean Dr. Schott wasn't in the back.

He shook his head. "I can't believe it. They're respected professionals. Even if they are a bit creepy. Vets stealing animals—it sounds like one of Jones's stories, doesn't it?"

"Yeah, but animals *are* disappearing. They have to be going somewhere."

She was absolutely correct. Something was definitely going on. But what? The image of Smokey's tail disappearing in the grass came back to him. Could she be involved? Could the nasty gray cat be working with the mountain lion? It was possible. Everyone knew cats were in league with one another.

A loud snore disturbed his thinking. Bunwinkle had fallen asleep. The stress of the day had finally caught up with her. She looked so small lying there.

They could've lost her today. Horace's stomach

turned to stone. The families of those missing animals must be sick with worry. Some of their loved ones had been missing for weeks.

The pet thieves had to be apprehended. Especially if they had their eyes on Bunwinkle.

"Help . . . help," she called in her sleep, her legs twitching as if she was trying to run.

Horace snuggled close to her, and after a few minutes she calmed down. No one was going to get his sister.

The next morning, bright and early, Bunwinkle put her snout in his ear and whispered, "Are you awake?"

"What do you want?" he grumbled. He hadn't slept well, waking up every few hours to check on Bunwinkle. And this was the thanks he received, her hot breath going in and out, in and out. It was maddening.

She hopped up onto the couch and in a chirpy voice said, "I knew you weren't asleep." She snorted loudly. "I want to find those animals and get those creeps who tried to pignap me."

Bunwinkle looked down and pawed at the

blankets. "Will you help me?" Before he could answer, she blurted out, "I promise I'll listen this time and I won't run off by myself."

Impossible. There was no way the little piglet would ever be able to control herself, and yet he couldn't say no. Yesterday had opened his eyes.

"Of course I'll help." Horace stood tall. "We're partners, aren't we?"

The smile she gave him lit up her face. "Really?"

He nodded. "Absolutely. Besides, we can't leave it to the humans. They'll never figure it out."

"That's right. And I already know what the pet-nappers smell like. Like cats and cleaning stuff."

"See, humans probably wouldn't even have noticed that. They have terrible sniffers. It's up to us to solve this mystery, Bunwinkle." Horace held up his paw. "Pet-tectives investigate?"

She hit it with her hoof. "Pet-tectives investigate!"

"Chow time," Eleanor called from the kitchen.

Horace's stomach rumbled. "I'm sure we'll be able to find clues much faster with full stomachs."

Bunwinkle nodded. "Totally."

* * *

When they finished eating, Horace led the way to the back porch. "I think we should start with the pond behind the barn."

Bunwinkle stared at him. "But I wasn't back there when it happened."

"That is true." He tried to look casual as he continued. "However, no criminal would remain at the scene of his most recent crime. Or attempted crime, in this case."

"You just want to see if the ducks are back, don't you?" Her voice was sour.

Horace glanced up at the clouds, down at his paws, over at the chicken coop. "Maybe."

"Fine," she grumbled, "but let's question them before we chase them away. They may have seen something."

Horace didn't reply. Questioning birds would be a waste of time. They were terribly foolish creatures. Take the chicks, for example—they still thought Bunwinkle was a rhinoceros.

As they rounded the barn, Horace heard the ducks quacking away. How dare they infest the pond again! Without thinking, he charged toward the water.

"Get out of here, you filthy brutes!" Horace shouted.

The small flock took to the sky, quacking rude things as they went.

Bunwinkle frowned at him so hard, her forehead wrinkled. If she'd folded her front legs, she would've looked exactly like Eleanor when one of the nanny goats knocked over the milk bucket.

"Horace! We were going to talk to them, remember?"

His face became hot and he couldn't meet her eyes. "Oh yes. That was unfortunate, what I just did."

A small smile curled her lips. "Say you're sorry."

"I apologize," he said with quiet dignity.

"What? I couldn't hear you," Bunwinkle teased.

She really was terribly immature. "I apologize."

In answer, she stretched out her tongue and licked him.

Horace froze, his ears burning with embarrassment. "What are you doing?"

She licked him again. "I'm getting the food on

your peaches."

"My what?" He hadn't eaten any peaches.

"Your peaches. You know, your cheeks, the white part next to your mouth. Where your whiskers grow. Ellie calls them peaches."

"Isn't that sweet?" a raspy voice called from the far side of the water.

Smokey.

Horace's heart sank.

The stray looked worse than she had the first time they met. Her gray fur was crusted with mud and hay, and part of her tail was charred. She smelled odd too, as though she'd bathed in hand gel. What had happened to her? She flicked her tail, and for the first time Horace noticed there was another cat sitting next to her.

He was tall and lean, with excellent posture. His white fur was immaculate, and he had an impressive dark gray mustache that stretched across his face and curled up at the ends.

What was a gentleman like that doing with Smokey?

"Greetings. I am Horace Homer Higgins III of the noble Boston Terriers." He placed a paw on his chest, then gestured to his partner. "This is Bun—"

"Oh, wow!"

Bunwinkle had discovered the mustache. It was obvious from the way she leaned in and stared at the white cat's face.

"Uh-hmm." Horace cleared his throat, hoping to get her attention, but it was no use. She was mesmerized.

"Excuse me," the white cat said in a high-pitched voice. "Don't you know it's rude to stare?"

"Dude, you have an awesome 'stache," Bunwinkle declared with admiration.

"Well! You really are the most thoughtless creature, aren't you? Don't you know it's impolite to point out a lady's flaws?"

Oh, not a gentleman, a lady.

"Flaws?" Bunwinkle wrinkled her nose. "Your mustache is amazing. You should be proud of it. I would be."

"Do you really think so?" The white cat put a paw up to her face.

Bunwinkle nodded. "Oh, yeah."

"Well, thank you. I suppose I should introduce myself. My name is Princess Sofaneesba."

"No, it ain't." Smokey moved between them, an ugly smile on her ugly face.

"Smokey, please," the princess pleaded.

"What's the matter, Princess? Don't want these idiots to know your *real* name? Don't want anyone to know you're named after a weirdo artist obsessed with watches?" Smokey turned to Bunwinkle. "Her humans called her Dalí. But this

simpleton here thought her name was Dolly—
right up until I showed her his picture."

Princess Sofaneesba's head hung down. It
looked like she was trying not to cry.

Bunwinkle moved closer to her. "It's okay. I
think both names are awesome."

"Oh yeah?" Smokey continued. "And what's
your name? Pork Chop? Bacon? Or should I just
call you Breakfast?"

Bunwinkle tilted her chin up and said, "My
name is Bunwinkle. And it was given to me by my
human. Do you have a family, or are you a stray?
'Cause you look like you sleep in weeds and roll in
cow pies."

Smokey hissed and arched her back. Princess
Sofaneesba raced behind a bush.

The stray cat crouched low, ready to spring at
Bunwinkle, but the piglet stood her ground. She
was going to get hurt. Horace couldn't let that
happen. Without thinking of the consequences,
Horace raced between them.

"Don't do it, Smokey!" he snarled.

Smokey turned and glared at him. "Who's
going to stop me? You? I've seen bigger loaves of

bread."

Horace growled and edged closer to her, ears back, teeth bared.

Smokey yowled in his face, but he didn't flinch. Her expression turned hateful. They stared at each other until she spat at him.

"I'll remember this, Horace."

"You'd better."

Horace stood tall as the gray cat stalked away. There'd be trouble later, he was sure of it. Smokey would never let this insult pass. He'd won today, but he'd have to be on his guard in the future.

Once she was off the property, he swung around to check on Bunwinkle and Princess Sofaneesba. They wore the same amazed expression: eyes wide, mouth hanging open.

Bunwinkle ran over. "That was awesome, Horace. You totally protected us. You're like a superhero."

He blushed. "No, no."

The princess smiled at him. "You were so brave."

"Well . . . maybe a little."

She really was a charming individual. For a

cat, that is.

"How did you meet Smokey?" Bunwinkle asked the question Horace had been thinking.

"We moved here a little while ago and I didn't know anyone. Smokey was sitting outside the house one day when I went for a walk. She was ever so friendly and quite humorous at times. I liked her a great deal." The cat sighed deeply. "But once I invited her into my home, she changed. First, it was little rude comments about my humans.

"Once she found out about my name . . . well, it went downhill from there. One day she actually scratched Papa, so he removed her from the house permanently. After that, she became positively vicious. I kept hoping her behavior would improve, but of course it didn't."

Smokey's behavior would never improve. She was mean to the core. Attacking humans and other animals without . . . Wait, attacking other animals? Smokey was the one behind the disappearances!

It made sense—Bunwinkle had smelled cat fur in the field, and Horace had seen Smokey there that day. Well, he'd seen her tail. And today she'd smelled of hand cleaner.

He was vaguely aware of Bunwinkle asking the white cat, "And . . . um . . . how did you come up with that name? Princess Softball?"

"Sofaneesba."

"Yeah, that."

"I picked it out of a book," the princess said proudly.

"You know, Princess Sofa Cushion . . ."

"Sofaneesba."

". . . is a great name. Isn't it, Horace?"

He nodded, although he wasn't sure what he was agreeing with. He wasn't paying attention to their conversation. He was thinking about Smokey.

"Thank you, small pig. You've been most kind. I wish there was something I could do for you."

Horace lifted his head. "Maybe there is. You said your human cast Smokey out of your house, correct? How long ago was that?"

A thoughtful look settled on the white cat's face. "Three weeks. I remember because it happened the day of that big rainstorm."

Bunwinkle gave him a curious look. "What're you thinking?"

He bent his head close to her ear and whispered, "Do you remember when the animals started disappearing?"

Understanding bloomed in her eyes. "About three weeks ago! You think Smokey's our culprit?" she said in what she thought was a whisper but was actually a shout.

"What is it you think she's done?" the princess asked with a sigh.

"She's taking animals that don't belong to her." Bunwinkle tapped her hooves excitedly.

"Taking animals? Why on earth would she do that?"

Horace put a paw to his chin. "Perhaps she's forcing them to give her food. Or perhaps she's jealous, and keeping animals away from their families makes her feel better."

"Perhaps," Bunwinkle cut in, "she's a big jerk and likes to hide animals away for the fun of it." Her eyes lit up. "Hey, I bet we could track her. I'm gonna do that right now." She put her snout to the ground and started sniffing.

Horace and the princess watched as Bunwinkle sniffed her way into the tall grass behind the barn.

Sofaneesba was quiet for a moment before she asked, "Were they all pets from this neighborhood?"

"Yes," Horace answered.

"Do you know if they've been hurt?"

He shook his head slowly.

"I don't believe Smokey would do something like that. At least I hope she wouldn't. But if she did, I might have an idea where she took them. I need to check something first. I'll meet you here tomorrow morning to share what I find."

"Be careful. Don't take any unnecessary chances," Horace said, and was rewarded with a gracious smile from the princess as she took her leave.

As soon as the cat rounded the corner of the barn, Bunwinkle emerged from the grass and announced, "Nothing in there." She looked around. "Aw, I didn't get to say goodbye to Princess

Sopapilla."

"She's going to investigate something for us."

Bunwinkle nodded. "So, hey, I was thinking while I was in the grass, and you know what, I'm totally gonna grow a mustache."

Horace tilted his head. Was that even possible?

They woke bright and early the next morning so they could go down to the pond and wait for the princess. In truth, neither of them had slept well. Horace had worried that something would happen to their new friend, and Bunwinkle had checked her reflection every ten minutes to see if her mustache had grown in yet.

Horace circled the pond while Bunwinkle searched the underbrush on the far side. She returned with something in her mouth.

"What is that?" he asked, against his better judgment.

"I don no, bu iss sicky."

He closed his eyes. "Bunwinkle, you can't just put things in your mouth! Did you sniff it first? Test it with your tongue in case it's poisonous? There's a process you have to go through before you chew on something."

She shrugged and swallowed. "No worries, I'm totally fine."

What was he going to do? She clearly had no sense of self-preservation. He'd simply have to watch over her constantly.

They waited a long time for Princess Sofaneesba, and the longer they waited, the more concerned they became.

"Do you think something happened?" Bunwinkle asked.

Horace looked up from his legs. "I don't know."

He didn't want to alarm the piglet, but he had a heavy feeling in his chest that said something was wrong. Please let Sofaneesba be safe.

"Let's check her house. Maybe she's sick or she started a really good movie or something."

Before they could leave, Smokey stepped out of the shrubs, looking more ragged than ever. "You seen Princess What's-Her-Face?" she asked.

Bunwinkle glared at her. "Did you do something to her?"

A deep, wheezy laugh was the only reply.

Horace moved up beside Bunwinkle. "Did you

harm her?" he asked.

The gray cat narrowed her eyes at them. "I didn't touch her. Besides, I'm looking for her too. She promised me some food."

"I don't believe you!" Bunwinkle shouted. "What did you do to her?"

Smokey hissed at her. "Nothing compared to what I'm going to do to you."

The cat jumped at Bunwinkle. Horace threw his body between them, so instead of Smokey's claw colliding with Bunwinkle's tender belly, it caught Horace in the neck.

Blood dripped onto the ground. He spun around. That was it! He was through with this feline menace. He growled from deep inside his chest, and Smokey hissed back. He kept his eyes on hers, ready for her next attack. Then he heard the quacking.

Blast it! Those rotten birds were back.

"Horace, look out!"

6

Dr. Schwink

What a fight! Winkie had never seen anything like it. Horace never backed down, even after Smokey scratched his neck. He growled, and the gray furball launched herself at him. He ducked, and she flew over his back, right into the pond. It was awesome!

Smokey yowled and screeched, then scrambled out of the water.

"I'll get you for this!" she shouted.

"Like you got all those other animals? We know you did it, Smokey!" Winkie yelled back.

She turned to Horace and her excitement died. His peaches had lost their pink, and his eyes were scrunched together.

"We need to find Ellie," she said.

Horace nodded, then winced as blood oozed out of the scratches on his neck.

Winkie's stomach flip-flopped. They had to find their human *quick*, before Horace passed out or Winkie threw up.

They found her feeding the chicks with the Hogland twins. She hurried out of the coop as soon as she saw them.

"Oh, baby boy, what happened?" She dropped to her knees and checked Horace's wounds.

He whimpered when she touched his neck. Winkie pressed her side to his, wishing she could help.

"Is he okay?" the freckled twin asked, her eyes as big as plates.

"I'm sorry, girls, we're not going to be able to feed the chicks together today. I've got to get Horace to the vet."

The girls left the coop with identical worried faces. "Can we help?"

Ellie shook her head. "I don't think so. You should probably head home."

They clasped hands and nodded.

As they walked away, Ellie turned to Winkie. "What about you? Are you okay?" She gently ran her hands over Winkie's body. When she was done, she sighed. "Thank heavens."

After that, Ellie went into super-speedy mode. She ran into the house and came back with her purse and a dish towel. She bandaged Horace's neck and rushed him to the car. Winkie chased after her. No way was she staying home. Horace needed her.

The vets' office was busy when they walked in. The waiting room was packed. Humans sat in every seat, and animals sprawled all over the floor.

They checked in and then sat down to wait. Ellie held Horace the whole time. He kept his eyes closed and his body curled up tight in her arms. There was nothing for Winkie to do except worry. And chew on the leg of the chair.

What if something happened to Horace? Sure, he was snooty and a know-it-all, but he always took care of her. He'd even apologized after he'd chased the birds. She glanced over at him shaking in Ellie's arms.

Please let him be all right.

She moved closer and pressed her cheek to his. That's when she noticed the announcement board. The ads were all gone. Now it was completely covered in missing-animal posters. The old posters were still there, but four more had been added, including one for a goat. As she read over the new flyers, a woman walked in.

"My cat's gone missing. I checked with animal control and they haven't seen her, but they thought you might have. She's white and has a dark gray mustache."

Winkie whipped her head around to see if Horace had heard. His eyes were open and focused on the lady at the counter.

"I'm sorry—we haven't seen any cats like that. You're welcome to put a flyer on our board, and I'll let everyone here know to keep a lookout for her."

"Thank you." The woman's voice was soft and high, like the princess's.

At the door, the woman took off her glasses and wiped her eyes.

So the princess really was missing. No matter what that rotten Smokey said, Winkie knew she had something to do with it.

"We've got to stop Smokey," Horace growled. "She's out of control."

"Horace?" the tech called out. "Dr. Schwink will see you now."

Their exam room was at the far end of the building. And it was freezing. Winkie started shivering as soon as the tech opened the door.

"Sorry about the room. We don't use it for examinations very often," the tech said. "You usually see Dr. Schott, but he's got his hands full with a bulldog at the moment, and we wanted to get you in right away."

Ellie set Horace down on the counter so the tech could check him out.

"These don't look *too* bad to me, but Dr. Schwink still needs to check them." She picked up her tablet, typed a few things, and then left.

Winkie moved next to Ellie to keep warm, but she didn't stay there long. What was she doing sitting there when Princess Soap Opera was in danger?

"It'll be all right," Horace said softly. "We'll find her."

He was right. It was like the Case of the Missing Keys—they would find her, because no one else could.

She leaned against Ellie's leg again and waited for the vet to come. When the door finally opened, a tall, bald man walked in.

"*Meine Güte!* It's bitter in dis room." He fiddled with something on the wall, and the cold air stopped blowing. "Dat should help, but also I vill leave de door open a bit. I don't tink we have to worry about dese little pets running avay."

He held out his hand to Ellie. "I'm Dr. Schvink. I understand your little doggie got in a fight vith a kitty cat. Is dat so?"

Ellie nodded.

He typed something on his tablet, then peeked at Horace over the top of it and wrote some more.

This guy was just as big a weirdo as Dr. Shot.

Dr. Schwink finally finished making notes. "Good. Now I make my exam." He washed his hands, twice, then put on a pair of gloves. "You vill be a good boy, ja?"

Winkie moved to the other side of the room before he could peel back the towel. She did not

want to see it again. Just thinking about the blood
made her stomach flip-flop.

"Not the tail! Not the tail!"

Winkie's head snapped around. "Horace?"

It wasn't him. But he'd heard the voice too. His
ears had perked up, and he had a funny expression on his face.

Where was it coming from?

"My tail!" the voice cried out again.

It got louder as Winkie moved closer to the open

door. Maybe she should check it out. She looked over her shoulder. The humans weren't paying her any attention. She could sneak out and be back before they knew she was gone.

But it didn't feel right to leave Horace.

"Why? *Why?*"

Winkie's eyes met Horace's. She jerked her head toward the door. He nodded and whispered, "Pet-tectives investigate."

Winkie stood up tall. Time to be brave like her brother.

She gulped, then forced herself to follow the sound of crying. It led her down a dark hallway. Winkie didn't have great eyesight, but she could smell a potato chip from a mile away and she could hear the can opener from the pond. So even though she couldn't see her hoof in front of her snout, she knew she was close to a whole bunch of animals.

Very close. She pressed her ear to the door next to her.

"My tail."

"My eye."

"Nobody knows the troubles I've seen."

Yeah, this was definitely the place. Winkie look at the sign on the wall. It read **RECOVERY**.

She pushed on the door with her hoof, and it swung open to show a large room filled with suitcases. The door swung shut before she could get a better look.

Suitcases? That couldn't be right.

She hit the door again and raced into the room. As the door shut, the lights dimmed.

Great.

"My eye!" The shout came from the suitcase right in front of her.

Winkie's whole body started shaking. This had been a bad idea. Maybe she should go back to Horace and Ellie.

She turned back to the door, then stopped. Wait, what would Suey do? Would she run back to Andie when she got scared? No, she would investigate, and that's what Winkie would do too.

Winkie crept closer to the suitcase to get a better look.

It wasn't a suitcase. It was a kennel. On the side was a heart-shaped sticker that read **BE GENTLE WITH ME, I HAVE MEOWIES.** She peeked into a cutout on the side. A cat paced back and forth, muttering something she couldn't quite understand. Then, without warning, he turned and looked at her with his *one eye*.

Where his other eye should have been there was a huge bandage.

"They took my eye. Couldn't see much out of it anymore and it oozed green goop, but it was still my eye."

Green goop? Agh.

"Who took your eye?"

But the cat wasn't paying attention to her. He was too busy shredding the bandage covering the right half of his face. No way was she gonna hang out to see what was underneath. Winkie scurried away to the next kennel. There was a happy-face sticker on this one: **DON'T TAKE MEOWT. I'M NOT WELL YET.**

The cat inside was passed out on her side, drool dribbling out of her mouth. Her leg was in a splint.

Winkie moved on to the next and the next. Most of the animals were asleep. The few that weren't stared at her with glazed eyes. All of them had bandages or braces. Someone had operated on them.

She shivered. This place gave her the heebie-jeebies. And the little stickers with their cheery sayings only made it creepier.

At the end of the first row she found the one who'd led her there. A black cat sat staring at a bandaged stub on her rear end.

"My tail, my beautiful tail." She turned her head and caught sight of Winkie. "Look what they did to me."

Winkie moved closer. "What happened?"

The cat sighed dramatically. "It was terrible. I'd followed my human into the room where she cleans herself and uses the human litter box. I wanted to stare at my beautiful face in the mirror. But my human wouldn't allow it. She closed the door to keep me out. Pain shot through my tail and straight up my back. Everything is a blur after that. I don't even know how I got here."

Winkie's heart beat faster. Boy, she needed to chew on something in the worst way.

"What am I to do? How will I keep my balance? How will I express the full range of my emotions?"

The cat put her head in her paws and sobbed.

"Can I ask you one question?"

She lifted her head. "It's midnight."

"What?"

"You wanted to know the name of this tragic creature you see before you. Well, it's Midnight."

Winkie rolled her eyes. What a drama queen!

"Midnight. Got it. So, Midnight, who removed your tail?"

The sobbing started up again. "Those monsters in the white coats."

Aha! Smokey wasn't behind the petnappings. It was these no-good, shot-giving, weird-sounding fiends. And Winkie was going to stop them.

"Hey. Hey, piggy."

The deep voice came from a kennel closer to the door. It belonged to a yellow Lab. His kennel was bigger than the others, giving the big dog room to stretch his legs out, which was good since he had splints on two of them.

"Hi, I'm Winkie."

"Name's Samuel Adams."

"Samuel Adams? Hey, is your human John Adams?"

MISSING

NAME: KODIAK
EYES: BLUE   WEIGHT: 70 lbs

The dog tilted his head, his forehead wrinkled.
"No, Trevor is my human."

"Oh." Winkie stared at the hip-to-paw casts on
Sam's hind legs. "What happened to you?"

"No idea. One minute I was playing, and the
next minute I was rolling on the ground in pain.
Next thing I knew, I was here."

"That's terrible."

He nodded. "Yeah. I mean, Trev and I were on
our way to becoming the top frizball team in the

state! You've heard of frizball, right?"

She shook her head.

"It's the number one canine-human competitive field sport."

Winkie stared at him. None of that meant anything to her.

He shrugged. "It's kind of a big deal."

"If you say so."

They stared at each other for a moment. Then Winkie asked, "Do you have any idea what's going on here?"

Sam shook his head. "Not really. But it's not a safe place, that's for sure. Animals come and go at all hours, and we never see them again. Body parts disappear. Look at that cat you were just talking to."

They both looked over at Midnight, who kept staring at what was left of her tail.

"Who knows what these doctors are up to? I don't trust them one bit. And neither should you. You need to get out of here before they come back."

Winkie's tummy flip-flopped. "Thank you, Samuel Adams." She turned and ran for the door.

What would those evil vets do to her if they caught her in there? She smacked the door with her hoof, and there stood Kissy Face Lady. She narrowed her eyes at Winkie.

"What are you doing in here?" All trace of the fun, friendly lady from earlier had disappeared. She came toward Winkie, a mean look in her eyes.

Uh-oh. The tech was in on it.

Winkie took off, diving between the lady's legs and escaping through the door before it closed.

Angry Face Lady chased her down the hall and into the exam room.

Dr. Schwink was washing his hands at the sink as Ellie cradled Horace in her arms when Winkie burst into the room, the tech right on her tail.

"You'll never believe where I found this one." She grabbed for Winkie.

"Hey, be careful!" Ellie snapped.

"Your pig was in the postsurgery center. We try to keep it sterile to minimize the risk of infection. Now I'll have to go through and clean everything again." Winkie hid behind Ellie's leg, her body shaking.

"I'm so sorry. We're all a little out of sorts because of this."

Dr. Schwink stepped forward. He stared down at Winkie with cold eyes. "You have been a naughty girl. If you vere my piggy, I'd keep you on a leash so you'd never get avay from me."

Oh no. She had to get out of there. Winkie's body tensed.

"Okay." Ellie jumped in. "Well, we're leaving now, so you won't have to worry about us anymore."

She picked up Horace and nodded her head at Winkie. "You stay with me, do you hear?"

After what she had just seen in that back room, Winkie didn't plan on leaving Ellie's side ever again.

As they drove away, she whispered to Horace, "I have so much to tell you."

7

A Real Mystery

Horace snuggled down into his blankets on the couch while Bunwinkle told him about the horrors she'd witnessed.

"It was awful, Horace. This one cat was missing an eye. She started to rip off her bandage so she could show me, but I got out of there. And this other cat, they cut off the tail. She showed me the stump and everything. And then—"

"No." Horace held up a paw. "No more. My stomach can't handle it."

He shifted to get comfortable and pain shot up his neck. He winced. These wounds were a dreadful nuisance.

Bunwinkle hopped up. "Here, let me help."

She pawed at the blankets until she'd practically knocked them both off the couch.

"Th-that's good," Horace said. "I feel much better now, Clara."

"I'm not Clara—I'm Winkie." Her eyes grew round. "Oh no. Did you lose your memory?"

If he hadn't been so uncomfortable, Horace would have laughed. "I know who you are. I was paying you a compliment. Clara Barton was a nurse during the Civil War. She founded the Red Cross."

"Let me guess. She was from New England."

"Of course."

Bunwinkle smiled, then jumped down again.

"We have to do something, Horace!" She paced back and forth in front of the couch, an angry frown on her face. "We gotta stop those evil vegetarians."

"Veterinarians," he corrected her automatically.

It didn't make sense. Why would respected professionals steal animals and do horrible things to them? If it were *one* of them, say that dreadful Dr. Schott, Horace might be able to believe it. But they would all have to be in on it, and he just couldn't believe that.

"Did you see any of the pets from the missing posters?"

Bunwinkle's nose wrinkled up as she thought. "I guess not." She gave him a suspicious look. "You believe me, right?"

"I believe you saw wounded animals, yes," he replied.

"What does that mean?" She put her front legs on the couch and glared at him.

He heaved a heavy sigh. "It means I'm not convinced the vets are our culprits. I still think it's more likely that Smokey is behind the petnappings."

"No way. You're just saying that because she scratched you."

"I'm saying that because the evidence against Smokey is the strongest. First piece of evidence: you smelled cat fur and hand gel before you were chased in the field."

"Yeah, but the vets smell like that too, 'cause they treat cats all day and they gotta wash their hands afterward. And you saw their van drive by at the same time." Bunwinkle shot him a smug smile.

"Dr. Schwank was taking care of the Hogland horse. That's why he was in the neighborhood," Horace countered. "Smokey lives here."

"Oh yeah. What's her motive? Why would she steal animals?"

"Jealousy. She doesn't have a home, so she's taking pets away from theirs."

"That doesn't make any sense." Winkie stomped a hoof. "And what about that missing goat? Smokey may be mean, but she's not big enough to capture an animal that size."

Horace refused to back down. "The goat probably ran away on its own. We don't know for sure that all the animals on those flyers were stolen. Or it's possible Smokey had help from the mountain lion. Cats are notorious for traveling in packs."

Bunwinkle's nostrils flared. "What about the animal experimentations?"

He narrowed his eyes at her. "Necessary medical procedures."

"It's the vets. I'll prove it."

"No you won't, because I'm going to prove it's Smokey."

They stared at each other until Eleanor came in to check on Horace. After she replaced his bandage, she hugged the two of them close.

"Bunwinkle, you look after your brother, okay?" She turned to Horace. "And you look after your sister. I don't know what I'd do if something happened to either one of you." She dropped kisses on their heads. "I'm off to pick up feed for the chicks. Love you guys."

Horace sighed. Eleanor was right. They *were* family now, and family cared for one another. It surprised Horace how much that meant to him. Plus the piglet would never leave behind her uncivilized ways without his constant supervision.

He cleared his throat. "I'm not ready to look for clues right now, but we could watch those detective shows you like, if you want."

"Okay, I guess." She snuggled next to him and started gnawing on the frame of the couch. "Too bad we don't have popcorn."

Later, as he was drifting off to sleep, he heard her say, "I'm still going to prove it's the vets."

By morning Horace's neck was much better, and he was ready to prove his theory about Smokey. He'd hoped his partner would come to her senses, but she woke up more determined than ever to prove her theory.

"We need to go to the field across the road, where the vets almost got me. There will definitely be clues," she said.

"But it's not safe. You said so yourself. We can investigate the pond area where we last saw Smokey."

Bunwinkle narrowed her eyes at him. "You're just scared of leaving the Homestead."

Horace sat up straight, and with all the dignity he possessed, he said, "Eleanor told us never to leave the property. Those are the rules. And since I am a good dog, I obey the rules. Unlike some piglets I could name."

"You know what? I'll go by my—"

Horace's stomach twisted, remembering the

last time they'd had a conversation like this. How Bunwinkle was chased through the field. No matter how much she frustrated him, he wanted her to be safe.

"No," he said. "We stay together."

Her mouth turned down. "Fine. I'll go to the pond with you, but only if you promise to search the field with me afterward."

"Glad to see you're being reasonable."

She stuck out her tongue as she passed by.

The pond provided several interesting pieces of evidence. First, the ducks had returned, which irritated Horace to his core. How many times did he have to shoo them away? Second, there were signs of a struggle, and an interesting smell—hand sanitizer, animal fur, and something sweet, possibly cookies—lingered near the horse paddock. Third, and most important, they found a pet-grooming brush that hadn't been there the day before. It had the Schott, Schwink, & Schwank logo, which was enough for Bunwinkle to start gloating.

"Told you so," she said with a smug smile.

"It doesn't prove anything," Horace argued.

"They give those away at the first exam. And it looks like someone wrote on the handle."

Bunwinkle tilted her head. "How can you tell? It's all chewed up."

It was Horace's turn to smile smugly. "Which obviously means Smokey got to it. She's our culprit, all right."

"Oh, come on. Anyone could've chewed on it. Sniff it and see. It'll smell like those rotten vets."

Horace wrinkled his nose. "I try not to sniff anything in this area. It's downwind of the barn." His ears sprang up. "Speaking of the barn, perhaps Smith and Jones saw something. Were they out yesterday?"

"Supa erwy. Day were alweady back in da bawn when we got out hewr." Bunwinkle slurped on something.

"What's in your mouth?"

Her eyes shifted away. "Nofing."

"Spit it out."

Bunwinkle wrinkled her nose at him, then opened her mouth. A pile of pebbles poured out.

Horace stared, eyes wide. "You're lucky you didn't choke."

"They weren't very chewy anyway." She shrugged. "Now, what about the horses?"

"I think we should speak with them. They're possible witnesses." Horace was proud he remembered that phrase from *Andie's Adventures*.

Bunwinkle slouched down. "Do we have to? They hate me."

"Nonsense. They simply don't know you."

Eerie music filled the barn when they walked in. A moment later a human voice said, "Keep an eye out for visitors from other worlds."

Horace stopped. Where was that voice coming from?

"Is someone here?" Bunwinkle called.

They rounded the haystacks just as Smith hit the power button on the radio with his muzzle.

It all made sense now. The mysterious music that first day. Jones's wild theories. Horace had always wondered how an old barn horse knew so much about sprites and ghosts. Now he understood—they'd been listening to the radio.

Smith put on an innocent expression and greeted them. Jones didn't even pretend. He took one look at Bunwinkle and jumped back with a scream. "No winkies!"

"Really, Jones! Bunwinkle has behaved as properly as she's capable in yo—" Horace trailed off when he saw the look on her face.

"I've got an idea." She grinned at him, then stepped closer to Jones's stall.

"There's something I need to tell you, Mr. Jones."

The horse turned his head away. "La, la, la. I cannot hear the little pig sprite talking. She will not lead me away to my doom. La, la, la."

Bunwinkle kept talking. "Look, I wasn't supposed to say anything, because my mission is top secret. But I can't have you blowing my cover, either. So here's the deal: I'm a part of P.I.G."

Jones neighed, "I knew it. You're part pig and part demon creature, aren't you?"

"No, I'm *all* pig. But I also happen to be a part of the Paranormal Investigation Group. P.I.G. I'm here to look into recent paranormal activity." She glanced over at Horace and winked.

He *tsk*ed his tongue. How childish. Making up stories was no way to conduct an investigation. He would have to take over the questioning himself.

But just as he opened his mouth, Jones whispered loudly, "You said you're with P.I.G.?"

Bunwinkle nodded solemnly.

The old horse slowly inched his way to the front of the stall, eyes narrowed in suspicion. He stared at her a moment. Then he leaned down and stuck out his tongue. "Thee dat?"

"Yeeahhh."

"Horrible, isn't it?"

Bunwinkle and Horace shared a confused look.

Jones sighed deeply. "It's the bluetongue. I just know it."

"The blue . . . what?" Horace asked against his better judgment.

"The blue tongue. My tongue has turned a deep midnight blue. Obviously I'm diseased and about to die."

Bunwinkle leaned over to Horace and whispered, "Does it look blue to you?"

"No," he whispered back. "And isn't bluetongue a sheep disease?"

Jones whinnied. "Just gonna wither away and die, I guess."

Horace rolled his eyes. Sometimes Jones was just too much. Under his breath he whispered, "We need to ask them some questions."

"Hold on," Bunwinkle whispered out the side of her mouth. To Jones she said, "Mr. Jones, before you pass over to the other side, could you answer a few questions for us?"

The old gray horse sighed dramatically. "I suppose."

Horace jumped on a bale of hay so he wouldn't have to shout.

"Were you out in the paddock yesterday morning?" he asked.

"Yeth." Jones stuck his tongue out again. Probably to see if it was still blue, which it wasn't. Not that Jones would believe that.

Bunwinkle scrambled up next to Horace. "This is real important, Mr. Jones. A friend of ours was catnapped. Did you see anything? Like maybe a creepy red-haired guy?"

"Or Smokey the cat," Horace added.

Jones pulled his tongue back in, and a serious look came into his eyes.

"I saw who took your friend."

"It was Dr. Schott, wasn't it?" Bunwinkle turned to Horace. "I told you it was the vets."

The old horse raised his head and pivoted his ears as though he was worried about being overheard. When he was sure no one could hear them, he stretched out his neck and whispered, "It was aliens."

Horace put a paw to his head. He was getting a headache.

Bunwinkle's excited nodding quickly turned to head shaking. "No. Not aliens, vetritarians."

Horace didn't bother correcting her.

"But it *was* aliens." Jones stomped his hoof. "They watch us through the holes in the wall. Don't they, brother?"

Smith stopped scratching his neck on a post and nodded. "Don't care for red delicious apples myself. But my brother loves them."

The three of them stared at the spotted horse until he returned to his scratching.

"It's *true*. I've seen them. Short. Gray. Wrinkly," Jones insisted.

"Dr. Schwink!" Bunwinkle tapped her front hooves quickly. "Horace, that's totally Dr. Schwink."

Oh, for pity's sake.

"No, that is not 'totally' Dr. Schwink," said Horace. "It's nothing like the man. He's tall and bald." He turned to Jones. "And it wasn't aliens either. It was Smokey the cat."

"No, sir. I know what that cat looks like, and it

wasn't her. It was aliens. Tell you something else: one peeked in at me with its single beady eye. And . . . and they talk to Mal. I've heard them. It's all gibberish to me, but that varmint understands them."

"Mal the billy goat?" Horace asked, his stomach sinking. He'd met the goat once, and it had been quite memorable.

"That's the one. He sold all us critters out to the aliens."

"Are you sure it wasn't a bald guy with a funny accent?" Bunwinkle asked, clearly not ready to let the vets off the hook yet.

Horace shook his head. If there was one thing he'd learned from all those detective shows, it was that you had to follow the evidence. And the evidence said it was Smokey.

"Aliens!" Jones insisted, almost as if he could read Horace's thoughts.

Bunwinkle shimmied off the hay bale, a sour look on her face.

Horace leaned in to say thank you, but the old horse spoke first. "Be careful out there, young fella. Those creatures are looking to take us all. Watch out for the ray guns."

Bunwinkle waited for him on the other side of the hay bales, chewing on something. She spit it out and covered it with some loose hay.

"I still say it's the vets. Jones is an unreliable witness. Let's go talk to this Mal and get his statement."

Horace groaned. Why did Mal have to be a witness? If Winkie thought *Jones* was unreliable, wait until she tried to talk to the billy goat.

"We don't need to speak with Mal. He's—"

"Gonna back up my suspiciousness about the vets."

Before Horace could answer, a loud thud came from the stall at the far end of the barn.

"What was that?" Bunwinkle glanced around.

"Mal," Horace said with a sigh.

"Well, let's go talk to him." She trotted over.

He followed her even though he knew it was sure to end badly.

They stood in front of the stall while Bunwinkle

tried to interview the goat.

"Mal, it's Bunwinkle. Did you see who took the white cat with the awesomest mustache in the world?"

No response.

"It wasn't aliens—it was the vets." She moved closer to the door. "Right?"

There was another thud. The latch gave out and the stall door sprang open, hitting Bunwinkle in the face. She sailed past Horace and landed in a heap.

"Och, who dares to disturb Malcolm Mac-Goat?"

Before Horace could move, the mad goat marched over to Bunwinkle and nudged her with his muzzle. She scowled at him, then rolled on her side and bit him on the shin.

The goat jerked back. "Och. So it's a fight ye be wanting?"

Bunwinkle scrambled to her feet.

"Well, lassie, yer about to meet my NOGGIN!" Mal bellowed as he charged the little pig.

Horace watched in horror as their heads crashed together and Bunwinkle sailed through the air again. This time she landed in a loose pile of hay.

He moved to check on her, which turned out to be a mistake. As soon as he lifted his paw, Mal charged at him, shouting, "So yer going to help the wee peg, are ye?"

Horace sprinted off around the hay bales before the mad goat could catch him. "Stop it!" He called over his shoulder. "No one's attacking you. We're simply trying to ask a few questions."

"Oh aye? And that's why yon peg bit my leg?"

Horace was having trouble understanding

Mal. "Peg? No, we need to know about the aliens, I mean the eyes. I mean, we just want to know who's been taking the animals."

"Tell them what you've done, Mal!" Jones yelled from his stall. "Confess!"

The other animals chimed in too.

"Headbutt, headbutt," chanted the nanny goats.

From outside the chicks screamed, "Earthquake!"

And the alpacas laughed.

What a bunch of animals! If he survived this, he would never come back into the barn again.

Suddenly, from the top of the hay bales, Bunwinkle shouted, "Eat hooves, jerk face!"

Mal's eyes opened wide. "Yer off yer noggin, wee peg."

That's when the wee pig launched herself at the billy goat.

Horace expected the goat to move out of the way, but Mal froze. The billy goat's eyes rolled back in his head, and he started to fall over. Bunwinkle collided with his body on the way down and they hit the ground together with a loud *thunk*.

Her head popped up, a fierce gleam in her eyes. "That'll teach him."

"What in heaven's name is going on in here?" Eleanor stood by Smith's stall, hands on her hips. "Bunwinkle, leave Mal alone! Go sit by Horace."

Eleanor knelt by the billy goat's side and examined him. A few minutes later he came to and lurched to his feet. Eleanor walked him around a bit to make sure he was truly all right.

"Wee dog," Mal called out before he entered his stall. "It was nae aliens. Just a couple o' wee bairns."

"Wee barns? Does that make sense to you?" Bunwinkle asked once Mal was safely locked away.

Horace shook his head. It didn't make sense, but he had the feeling it should.

8

Dr. Schwank

Winkie was in a lot of trouble. Ellie put her in a time-out in one of the alpaca pens. Which was totally unfair. She hadn't really hurt Mal. He'd just fainted. Besides, he'd headbutted her first. Why wasn't he in trouble for that?

Maybe chewing would make her feel better. She dug around until she found something with just the right amount of crunch.

"What's in your mouth now?" Horace asked from the other side of the fence.

Winkie ignored him. She didn't need a lecture. She needed to chew her feelings.

"You might be interested to know Eleanor called Dr. Schwank. He'll be here tomorrow."

She spit out the thing in her mouth. "Good. We can inspect the van for traces of the princess and the others."

Horace didn't argue. He just got a weird look on his face.

Ellie appeared next to Horace and opened the gate to the pen. Before her human could change her mind, Winkie ran straight to the house.

Winkie didn't sleep well that night. Every time she closed her eyes, an image of the one-eyed cat from the vets' office popped into her head. She had to be on her guard against Dr. Schwank so he couldn't do that to her.

She was still awake when the mobile vet van pulled into the driveway the next morning. Winkie didn't like the look of it at all. No windows. What were they hiding in there? And it was perfectly clean. A van that drove around farm country all day should be covered in dirt.

She didn't like the look of Dr. Schwank either. You couldn't see any of him. He had a cap on his head and a surgical mask that covered most of his face. The only thing she could tell for sure about him was that he was tall.

"How are you doing, Pete?" Ellie asked when the vet got out of his van.

"Rough morning. Allergies are acting up, so I gotta wear this thing." He pointed to the mask. "The office flooded, and we spent the better part of the morning moving files and such. And then I just had to send off the Hoglands' old horse, Travere. Sad thing. The twins took it real hard."

"I'm sorry to hear that."

Dr. Schwank nodded. "Well, let's take a look at that goat of yours."

He followed Ellie across to the barn. At the door he turned and glanced back to where Winkie and Horace sat on the porch.

"Creepy," she whispered.

They waited until he walked into the barn, then raced to the van. They'd made their plan last night. They needed evidence, and the mobile van was the best place to look for it.

"Lucky he left the door open," Bunwinkle said, trying to climb up.

"He always leaves it open. Makes it easier to get supplies, I suppose." Horace boosted her into the van. Once she was in, he said, "I'll stay here and be the lookout. If someone comes out of the barn, I'll bark."

Sometimes Horace was the biggest chicken. "Fine."

The inside of the van was just as clean as the outside. And organized too. Everything important was either in a drawer or cabinet. Winkie pulled on a handle with her teeth, and it opened.

Needles!

Winkie slammed the drawer shut.

Horace came around to the back of the van. "Not so loud."

"I found the shots."

He shuddered, then went back to his lookout post.

She went through the drawers one by one. There were a bunch of surgical tools and bandages. The last drawer she opened was full of pet-grooming brushes like the one they'd found by the pond. This was good, but it wasn't enough to prove the vets were the petnappers.

Near the driver's seat, she found a case. She pushed it over, and files spilled out.

"Horace!"

He came round to the back again. "What? I'm not a very effective lookout if I'm not actually able to look out."

"You've got to see this."

He shook his head but jumped into the van anyway. "What is it?"

"Files on the missing animals."

"What? All of them?" He opened the top one with his paw.

"Totally."

Horace narrowed his eyes at her. "Did you actually go through them?"

"Well, no, but—"

"I'm glad it's nothing serious." Ellie's voice sounded close.

Winkie turned to Horace. "You were supposed to be on guard duty."

He gave her an irritated look. "I would have been, but someone called me into the van."

They shoved the files back into the case and raced out of the van. Winkie was in such a hurry, she missed the last step and tumbled to the ground.

"Bunwinkle!" Ellie had Winkie in her arms in the blink of an eye.

"How are you doing, little one?" Schwank asked.

His voice was soft. Some animals might even have called it kind, but Winkie knew better. It was just an act. The whole thing was an act.

Ellie looked her over with a sigh. "You've got to slow down or you're going to get seriously hurt."

"Do you want me to give her a quick exam?"

"Would you?"

Dr. Creepy snatched Winkie up before she

could make a run for it. He ran his cold hands over her head, like Dr. Schott had done.

"Everything feels fine," the vet said, but he didn't put her down or hand her back to Ellie.

Winkie squirmed. She didn't trust this guy for a second. He was up to no good.

"Thanks, Dr. Schwank. She's a bit of a wild one," Ellie said, running a hand through her hair. "I don't know what to do with her sometimes."

"You know, in vet school they used to call me the pig whisperer. Can I try something?"

Ellie nodded, and the next thing Winkie knew, she was face-to-face with the evil vet. He pulled his mask down and then leaned in until their foreheads touched. He stared deep into her eyes. She tried to look away, but it was impossible. His eyes were light. So light, they looked almost white. Like they were made of ice.

She kicked and twisted. "Horace, help! He's trying to hippotize me."

"Shh," the vet whispered at her. "Stop wiggling. Be calm. Behave. Heal. Rest."

He said it over and over, and each time he said it, Winkie got tireder and tireder. Her eyelids were so heavy. So . . . heavy . . .

And then she was asleep.

Winkie woke up to find Horace's face an inch from hers. He looked worried.

"You're alive. Thank heavens!"

"What happened?"

"That dreadful Dr. Schwank mesmerized you. He told you to rest and you passed out. And another thing—Mal is missing."

"What?" Winkie stopped stretching.

Horace nodded. "He disappeared sometime last night."

"Last night? How long was I out?"

"Almost twenty-four hours."

Dang it! That creepy vet had put the whammy on her, and then he'd stolen Mal while she was asleep.

"You know what that means?" Horace asked.

"Yeah, those petnappers are going down."

He didn't laugh or give her a lecture. "No, it means Smokey isn't the guilty party. One animal couldn't get the better of that goat, even if she was the meanest cat in creation. And I don't think she'd hurt Princess Sofaneesba either. She'd never risk her meal ticket." He cleared his throat. "Bunwinkle, you were correct."

Winkie's jaw dropped. Horace had admitted he was wrong. Maybe he was sick. She put her snout on his forehead.

"What are you doing?"

"Checking to see if you have a fever." He didn't. He felt the same as always.

He pushed her away with his paw. "Very amusing. Now, if you're done playing, let's go get proof of the veterinarians' wrongdoings."

"How?"

"By interviewing eyewitnesses."

Winkie's face fell. "You mean the horses, don't you?"

"I do." Horace hopped off the couch and headed for the back door. "You coming?" he called over his shoulder.

Winkie followed him even though she knew it wouldn't do them any good. How were you going to get help from someone who believed in ghosts, aliens, and sprites, for pity's sake?

She caught up with Horace inside the barn door. "I think this is a job for Agent Bunwinkle."

"Oh, all right," Horace said with a sigh.

As they approached the stalls, they heard Jones's voice.

"This is it, brother . . . the end of the road. It's been a good life, hasn't it? You remember the tours we used to do? Boy, we sure had fun tossing those ole city slickers around, didn't we? Heh! And you remember that filly? The appaloosa? What was her name again?"

Smith didn't answer. His eyes were closed like he was asleep, but Winkie wasn't buying it.

"Sorry to interrupt, Jones, but I'm on urgent P.I.G. business," she cut in.

The old gray horse nodded his head. "I'm glad you came, Agent Bunwinkle. We don't have much time left, and I have a lot to tell you."

Maybe Horace was right. Maybe the horses did have something to say.

Winkie had never seen Jones look so serious. She put on her best listening face. "I'm ready."

"You were right: it wasn't aliens. I realized

that when they tried to take me."

"They?" Winkie and Horace asked at the same time.

Jones nodded solemnly. "They wanted to lead me to my new home, but they couldn't work the latch on my stall. So they took Mal instead."

"Well, who was it?" she asked. "Who took him?"

"Angels."

Winkie put a hoof over her eyes and groaned. What a waste of time. The vets were probably doing something horrible to their friends right now, and she and Horace were stuck talking to a loony.

Horace hopped up onto the hay bale closest to Jones. "Tell me about the angels."

What was he doing? He didn't actually believe this story, did he?

"Well, there were two of them. And they were small. They had the most beautiful halos."

"They were small?" Horace asked.

Jones nodded. "Oh yes. And they laughed a lot. It was enchanting. Just hearing it made me happy. And they'll be coming back for Smith and me real soon. Our time is running out, you see. You probably can't tell, but my brother and I are getting up there in age."

Winkie almost burst out laughing.

"Was Mal happy to hear them too?" Horace asked.

"No, sir. He fought the angels real hard. You know how it is, some critters just can't accept when it's their time to go. That's why I'm preparing myself. I want to be ready when the angels come for me."

Really?

"What about your brother? Did you see anything?" Horace shouted at the black-spotted horse in the next stall. Smith peeked at them through squinted eyelids and pretended to snore.

Jones answered for his brother. "He had that head cover on. The one that keeps the flies out. Says he can't see or hear a thing when it's on."

Winkie stared at Smith suspiciously. There was something fishy about that horse.

"Thank you, Jones." Horace climbed down from the hay.

"You're welcome. And it's been a pleasure knowing you. Both of you."

* * *

"I told you that wouldn't do us any good," Winkie said as they walked away.

Horace's face scrunched up the way it did when he was thinking hard about something.

"Maybe we should we talk to the nanny goats? They were outside, but they might have seen something."

"DON'T YOU DARE!" Jones suddenly shouted.

"Is something wrong with the nannies?" Horace turned back.

Jones laughed. "No, that was the name of that ole filly. Don't You Dare. She was quite a gal, wasn't she, Smith?"

"Let's get out of here," Winkie said.

The goats were no help. Minnie hadn't seen anything, and the other two laughed their faces off when Horace told them about Mal.

"Good riddance."

"Why would we want him back?"

Ellie walked out as they stood there. "Come on, guys. We'll drive around and look for Mal."

First stop was the goat's old home—MacDougal Farm.

"Och, haven't seen the beast since I sold him to ye," said the big man at the gate.

He sounded exactly like Mal. Maybe that was why the goat talked so funny.

After that they drove around for over an hour with no luck. Ellie stopped at every house, farm, and ranch along the route. The only place they didn't stop was the old barn around the bend from the Homestead. Even Mal couldn't get past a locked gate.

"He's not around here," Winkie muttered to herself. "He's in that back room at the vets' office."

The last stop was Hogland Farm. Ellie stopped at the big milking shed close to the main road. While she rolled down the windows, she stared at Horace and Winkie in the rearview mirror. "You two stay here. I'm going to talk with Lars for a minute. Do not get into *any* trouble. Do I make myself clear?" Ellie twisted around and gave them the stare until they started squirming. Then she got out and went into the shed.

Winkie stuck her head out the window as soon as Ellie closed the door. "Too bad we promised to be good. This is a great place to look for clues.

Dr. Schwank was here just before he came to the Homestead. He might have left some evidence." She watched the cows for a few minutes. "You know, I still can't believe the Hoglands don't raise hogs. It would make way more sense."

A loud sniff from Horace's direction made her turn. Her brother dog sat by the open window with tears pouring down his face.

Winkie rushed to his side. "What's wrong? Did something happen?"

"I think I've finally become countrified," he sniffed.

"What do you mean?"

"It doesn't smell bad to me anymore."

She turned her head so Horace couldn't see her grin.

Before long, Ellie and a tall, skinny man walked out of the milking shed together. He opened the car door for her, saying, "We'll keep a lookout for him, Eleanor. He's bound to turn up soon. Shoot, he might be back at your place already."

"Thank you, Lars. I hope you're right. I just . . . I can't imagine how he got out." Ellie shook her head.

On their way home, they passed the twins. The girls were walking up the road with a big bag hanging between them. They hopped up and down and waved when they saw Winkie and Horace.

"Too bad we didn't stop." Horace sighed. "I'm sure they had cheese for me."

9

Petnapped

They stayed up late going over the evidence. Winkie didn't know why—it was obvious the vets had done it. But Horace would not let it go.

"Something isn't right about this," he insisted.

She rolled her eyes. "I thought you agreed with me."

His forehead wrinkled. "I did, but the more we investigate, the more I question the veterinarians' involvement."

"You're thinking too hard."

Horace ignored her. "We know you smelled cat fur and hand gel in the field. We both smelled something sweet, like cookies. All the missing animals are from this neighborhood, which means the culprits must live in this area or spend a great deal of time here."

"Or they could've found them when they went to the vets' office," Winkie said.

"I don't think so. Smokey doesn't look like she's been inside a house, let alone a clinic, for quite some time." Horace nodded. "I think we can safely rule out a mountain lion attack at this point. A mountain lion would have gone for easier prey, and I'm certain Smith and Jones would have noticed one roaming around the barn. And we've already eliminated Smokey."

Winkie dropped her head on the blankets. "Yeah. It's definitely not them, 'cause it's totally the vets."

Horace got the teaching-moment look on his face. "But would anyone ever mistake them for angels?"

"Jones isn't the sharpest tack in the toolbox. He thought I was a sprite, remember?"

Horace shook his head and sighed. "I'm certain we're missing something."

"Yeah, sleep." Winkie yawned so hard, her jaw cracked.

"Goodness, how did it get so late? You should have said something."

For a second she thought about biting him. He must've noticed, because he suddenly smiled at her. "Let's get some rest. We can start again first thing tomorrow."

It was a bad night. Winkie had a hard time getting to sleep, and then she had weird dreams. Like the one where Dr. Schott was an evil scientist and he kept shouting, "Do what you like to me but you'll never find my bairn!" He said the word "barn" just like Mal did.

All of a sudden she was wide awake. The barn. That's what Mal had been talking about. There must be a clue in the barn. But they'd searched it already. Maybe something was behind it. Maybe there was some clue in the field back there. They needed to check it out right away.

"Horace." She nudged him with her snout.

"Leave this property, you loathsome devils."

She rolled her eyes. He was having the bird dream again. It was impossible to wake him up when he had that one. And he'd insist they check the pond first thing.

He'd be mad if she investigated by herself, but maybe she could clear the ducks out of the pond now. Then when he woke up, they could get right to work.

Everything was quiet and peaceful when she walked out. The ducks were back in the pond. Good thing she'd gotten there early.

She stopped to sniff the air. There was that smell again—animal fur and cookies and something like cleaning spray. Stronger than before. She heard rustling behind her . . . just before a pair of hands grabbed her and shoved her into a duffel bag.

"Horace! Help me!"

10

The Search Begins

Horace woke up late. He was used to Bunwinkle kicking him in the head around sunrise, but for some reason she hadn't done it today. He glanced around while he did his morning stretches. Her bed was empty and she didn't appear to be in the living room. She was probably eating breakfast.

"Morning, Bunwinkle," he said as he entered the kitchen.

Her bowl was full, but she was nowhere to be seen. Horace's chest tightened. Bunwinkle never left food in her bowl.

He walked over to his water dish, a frown forming on his face. Surely there was no reason to panic. She'd probably gone outside to take care of

her business. He nodded to himself. That was it. He'd give her a few minutes, then join her.

She wasn't outside either. He looked everywhere. Even under the porch, which was a filthy, spidery nightmare. She wasn't there. Maybe she'd fallen asleep somewhere. That was possible, right? She could be snoring away in

the barn, for instance, right now.

Horace could hear Jones's hysterical voice as soon as he walked in, and he froze for a moment.

"Something's wrong, Smith," Jones ranted. "I'm telling you. I can feel it in my bones. Something is very wrong."

He calmed down a bit when he saw Horace. "Oh, thank heavens! I was so worried." He tilted his head to look around Horace. "Wait, where's the little pig? Where is Winkie?"

"I don't know. I can't find her anywhere."

Jones's eyes opened wider and wider. He rocked against the door of the stall. "They took Winkie!" Jones cried. "They took her."

Horace's heart pounded. He'd known as soon as he saw that full bowl of food that something was terribly wrong.

"Who? Who took her?"

"The angels."

"No," Horace snapped. "No aliens. No angels. No more of your ridiculous stories. Bunwinkle is in danger. You have to help me!"

The gray horse dropped his head.

"That's enough, Horace," Smith cut in, frowning.

"My brother doesn't know who took her."

Horace shook his head, his panic growing by the second. The petnappers had gotten her, and he had no idea where to look.

"But *I* might know," Smith said quietly. "Heard a scream a while ago. Came from behind the barn. There might've been some laughter too. I think if you start by the pond, you'll pick up the scent."

Jones stared at Smith. "I thought you couldn't hear?"

"Well . . ." Smith stumbled over his words. "It . . . sort of comes and goes."

"You mean . . . ," Jones sputtered, "you've been pretending to be stone deaf for . . . what's it been? Five years?"

"Well, now."

"What else have you lied to me about?" Jones demanded. "Are we even brothers?"

11

They're No Angels

Worst. Day. Ever.

First she'd gotten pignapped, and now Winkie was stuck in some kind of cage—she couldn't see anything on account of the blanket covering it. *And* she was out of things to chew on. She'd torn the duffel bag to shreds as soon as she'd crawled out of it, and there was nothing else in the crate.

A lump formed in her throat, but she wouldn't let herself cry. Horace would figure out what had happened, and he'd come for her. And together they'd show those petnappers a thing or two.

Please, Horace, figure it out. Please. Please. Please.

Suddenly someone yanked the blanket off the cage. Winkie squinted, trying to get used to the light. Then she heard the door open. This was it— her chance to escape! Still half blind, she shot out of the kennel.

"Uh-oh, get her!"

Winkie knew that high-pitched voice. It belonged to someone she liked, someone she trusted. But who?

A small pair of hands grabbed at her. "Gotcha!"

Nuh-uh. Winkie squirmed and slipped away. I'm outa here.

She ran with all her strength, zigzagging around bales of hay and kennels. The other animals called out, but she couldn't stop. She had to find a way out. Her heart beat faster and faster as she ran.

Where was the door? The thieves were going to catch her again if she didn't find it. Maybe it was behind the big stack of hay.

Winkie squeezed between two bales and almost started crying—there was the door. She was almost free. She turned her head to check how close they were and got a good look at her captors for the first time.

White hair.

Freckles.

Overalls.

Winkie's mouth fell open and she tripped over her own feet. No way. The rotten, no-good jerks who'd petnapped half the neighborhood and thrown her in a bag . . . were the Hogland twins?

The freckled twin plucked Winkie up before she could run away again. "No more running away, Pigella Pigerina. We don't want you to get hurt."

"No, Linn, her name is Pigerina Pigella. Remember?"

"No, it's not. That's sounds silly."

Personally, Bunwinkle thought they both sounded silly.

"Oh, I just love that heart on her nose. I'm going to kiss it."

"No way!" Bunwinkle squealed.

The girls laughed, then planted smooches all over her face. Bunwinkle resisted at first, but that only made the little monsters laugh more and kiss harder. She stopped fighting. It was too late, they totally loved her now.

But she didn't enjoy the attention. Nope. And she definitely didn't tilt her head so they could kiss her ears. No, sir. She was just playing along until she could escape.

"Mama's going to want us back soon. Did you bring all the stuff? We need to get Pigerina Pigella ready."

Winkie shivered. Ready for what?

"You're going to be perfect, Pigella Pigerina."

12

Scent Hound

After the conversation with the horses, Horace rushed out to the pond—which was full of ducks. He didn't have time get rid of them at the moment, and from the smug way they stared at him while he put his sniffer to work, they knew it. He'd get them later.

He had Bunwinkle's scent. Now all he had to do was follow it. In circles around the pond. To the barn. Around the barn. Then to the garage and a pile of partially chewed things he refused to get close to.

Where could she be? If the vets really had taken her, she could be anywhere by now. It wasn't the vets, though. Horace knew it. The evidence simply didn't add up.

Please let her be safe.

He went back to the pond and started over. This time he wound up under the porch again, at another pile of Bunwinkle's treats.

Back to the pond again. The ducks laughed and quacked at him, but he ignored them. What was he going to do? Every time he searched for Bunwinkle, he wound up right back where he'd started from. A thought struck—what would Spot do? Spot would lie down, groom himself, and let his mind clear.

Horace dropped to the ground and began to lick his legs. He shut out the taunts from the rotten birds and pushed aside his fears.

Lick—finding Bunwinkle's scent was easy.

Lick—because it was everywhere.

Lick—but the thieves' scent wasn't.

Lick—so what he needed to do was search for a combination of Bunwinkle and the thieves.

Lick—which would smell like animal fur and something sweet.

Horace jumped up. Spot's method really did work. He put his sniffer down again. There was Bunwinkle's scent . . . and something more. He inhaled deeper. Now there was cat fur—the princess and Smokey, to be precise. Horace closed his eyes and opened his nostrils. This time when he sniffed, he caught it, a scent that was both familiar and unique—a rich aroma that made him smack his lips. It was . . . it was . . . cheese! That delicious, homemade kind the Hogland twins fed him.

The twins? Horace frowned. That couldn't be right. He put his nose down and inhaled again. It was easier to pick up their smell this time. He could hardly believe it, but the sniffer didn't lie. Those sweet little girls—who gave him treats and petted him—had taken Bunwinkle.

But why? Why take her? Why take any of the animals?

Those questions would have to wait. It was more important to find Bunwinkle, and the others, first. And now he knew that the animals had to be close by—the twins wouldn't be able to take them far. But where would they keep all of them? It couldn't be at Hogland Farm. Someone would've found them.

He'd have to follow the scent. He tracked it right up to the road in front of the house. It kept going, but he stopped. Eleanor had said never to leave the property. Horace looked back at the house, then at the road. He had no choice. Bunwinkle was in danger.

He followed the scent around the big bend in the road until he came upon a dirt road leading to an old barn, where local ranchers and farmers used to store hay. Paint flaked off the sides, the roof sagged, and the door to the hayloft hung from one hinge. It looked abandoned now. Eleanor had always avoided the place. She said it wasn't safe. But Horace was going to have to risk it, because that was where the scent led.

At the doors of the old barn, Horace braced himself. Who knew what horrors lay inside this building? The girls didn't seem mean, but they hadn't seemed like petnappers either. His heart beat fast. This must be how New England native and Revolutionary War hero Alexander Scammell had felt before he led the charge against the British at the Battle of Princeton.

He took a deep breath, then squeezed his body through a gap in the doors. He paused inside, listening for screaming or diabolical laughter, but all he heard were a few voices, murmuring softly.

He rounded the corner of the haystack in the center, and his jaw dropped. The barn was filled with animals, some in kennels and a few in pens.

He trotted over to a goat pen. At least he thought they were goats.

"Horace, is that ye?" the creature closest to him asked.

"Mal?" Horace tried not to stare, but it was difficult. Someone had covered the billy goat in red nail polish and shiny red ribbons. "Are you okay? Did they hurt you?"

"Och, nothin' can hurt this goat." He walked over to the gate. "But I could use yer help with this."

The latch on the gate was a simple thing. All Horace had to do was push a button with his head, and the gate swung open.

Mal turned to the other goats. "Come on, lads. Freedom!"

Horace jumped out of the way as the billy goats ran wild.

"Use yer noggins!" Mal shouted.

Time to move. Horace turned and bumped into a large kennel of cats. He recognized one of the cats right away.

"Princess! We've been so worried about you."

"Horace, how lovely. Do rescue us, please." She said it the same way she might invite someone to tea.

"Us?"

"You didn't notice who's beside me?"

The cat next to her had been shaved to look like a lion.

Horace laughed. "Looking good there, Smokey."

She hissed, then turned her back on him.

The latch on this kennel was too complicated for him. "I'm sorry, but I can't open it. But I'll be back with someone who can. After I find

Bunwinkle. Do you know where she is?"

Princess Sofaneesba shook her head sadly. "I'm afraid we don't. But the dogs might know. They've been here the longest."

Horace found the dog kennels on the other side of the hay bales. He approached one with a Husky in it. He stopped a few feet away. The smell of cheap cologne and hair spray was so strong, it made him dizzy. It tickled his sniffer too. He sneezed loudly.

"Bless you." The big dog's voice was deep and rumbly.

Even though it made his eyes burn, Horace

moved closer to the kennel. "Hello," he croaked.

"How's it goin'?"

Horace stared at the Husky through watery eyes. The dog's fur was shiny from all the hair spray, and there was a pretty, light blue ribbon tied around his neck. "You like it? It matches my eyes."

"Y-y-yes . . . ," Horace stuttered. "But how can you stand that smell?"

"It's called Night Wolf," the Husky replied, clearly offended. "And I happen to like it."

"Oh yes. Of course," Horace said, dabbing his eyes with a paw. "You haven't seen a small pig, by any chance?"

"Top of the hay bundles behind you."

"Thanks."

Horace glanced behind him. He'd completely missed the kennels on top of the hay. He climbed it by leaping from spot to spot. Halfway up he heard Bunwinkle's voice.

"No, I'm telling you, he said 'barns.'"

"I believe you're mistaken. He said 'bairns.' B-A-I-R-N-S." Horace didn't recognize the voice.

"Okay, so let's say he did say bairn. He was

still talking about this place, right?"

"No, no. You see, in Scotland the word 'bairn' means child. Malcolm was trying to tell you about the twins."

"Hmm. Okay, I get it now. It's kinda funny, when you think about it. The bairns are keeping the animals in the barn."

Horace's legs shook and threatened to give out under him. He leaned against the hay, relief flooding through him. Thank heavens she was alive and unharmed!

13

Rescue

Winkie was leaning back against the bars of the kennel, enjoying her little bairn-barn joke, when suddenly Horace popped up at the end of the hay.

"Winkie!"

"Horace!" Tears welled up in her eyes. "Am I ever glad to see you!"

He raced up her cage and licked her face through the bars.

"Stop," she giggled. "You're tickling me."

He pulled back from the cage and glanced over her. "Are you okay? You look . . . you look . . ." Horace paused.

"I know, I know. I'm wearing a tutu."

"And a tiara," Horace added.

"And a tiara," she agreed.

He cleared his throat. "Uh, hmmm, and lip-stick."

She leaned closer to Horace and whispered, "This is nothing. Check out Blue." She nodded her head at the dog sitting next to her.

The twins had really outdone themselves with *his* new look. They'd dyed his fur blue and some-how added silver glitter to the mix.

In a normal voice, Winkie said, "Hey, Horace, this is my friend Blue Sparkles. Blue, this is my brother, Horace."

Blue looked at Horace, then at Winkie. "Your brother?"

"We're adopted," she said.

Horace pawed at the lock. "I'll get you out of th—"

"You can't." Winkie stopped him. "You gotta have thumbs."

Horace squeezed his lips together so tight, his mouth looked like a straight line. He worked at the lock again, even though she'd told him it wouldn't do any good. She put her hoof on his paw.

"You have to get Ellie."

He looked like he wanted to argue, but then he shook his head and said, "I'll be back as soon as I can, I promise."

She smiled at him. "I know."

After Horace left, Winkie turned to Blue.

"Don't worry, Horace will have us out of here in no time."

Blue laughed. "Not me. I'm staying."

"What about your humans?"

"Are you kidding? I love it here!" He took a big bite of his food. "This is real steak they're feeding me."

14

Home Again, Home Again

Horace raced back to the Homestead. He ran through the house looking for Eleanor, but she wasn't there. Same thing with the barn and the garage.

Where was she?

He stopped running and stood in the center of the property, barking as loud as he could. Eleanor ran up from behind the barn. "Horace, thank goodness. I was so worried." She looked around him, just as Jones had done earlier. "Where's Bunwinkle?"

Now was the moment. He yipped at her, then ran back out to the road. He did it twice more before she figured out he wanted her to follow him.

The trip back was so much easier with Eleanor running alongside him. They paused in front of the old barn. Eleanor looked down at him. "She's in here?"

He scratched at the door as an answer. Eleanor nodded. "Okay." Then she pulled the chain off the handles and opened the doors.

They got about five steps in before Mal trotted up. "Och, don't forget yer billy!" he bleated loudly.

A huge smile spread across Eleanor's face. Her joy quickly turned to horror when she noticed the red goop all over him.

"Mal, are you all right?" She dropped to one knee and ran her hands over his body. It didn't take long for her horror to turn to confusion. "Is this . . . nail polish?"

He answered her with a gentle headbutt to her sternum.

Bunwinkle must have heard the commotion, because she squealed, "Ellie!" so loud it echoed around the old barn. Then Ellie dropped everything and scaled the hay bundles to get to her. "Oh, baby, what have they done to you?" She sat on the top bundle and unlocked the cage.

Horace could've cried. It was going to be all right.

"It's okay. You're safe now, little one," Eleanor promised, pulling Bunwinkle out and squeezing her close. Horace crowded in so he could lick his sister pig's face.

And that's when the twins walked in, pulling a red wagon full of food behind them.

"Let's give Blue Sparkles his treat first. He's going to love it."

"Linn? Nea? What are you doing here?" Eleanor asked.

The girls jumped and screamed, "Run!" But there was nowhere to go, because their mother blocked the way.

"I knew you two were up to something. You've been too . . . quiet. . . ." Her words trailed off as she looked around the barn. "What have you done?"

"Taken animals from the neighbors." Eleanor tucked Bunwinkle under her arm and climbed down the stacks of hay. She set Winkie on the barn floor next to Horace.

Horace nudged Winkie. "I told you it wasn't the vets."

She rolled her eyes.

Clary stared at Eleanor. "Eleanor? What are you doing here?"

"Apparently, I'm collecting my missing pig." Mal bumped her leg. "And goat. Isn't that right, girls?"

They looked at each other, then started crying. When no one moved to comfort them, they put their arms around each other.

"They're totally faking it," Bunwinkle whispered to Horace. "You can tell 'cause there's no tears."

And because they kept peeking to see if it was working.

Clary pulled the girls apart and turned them to face her. "I want to hear the whole story. Right now."

It was a good story. Actually, it was *several* good stories. According to Linn, it all started when they found a poor, defenseless dog lying on the dirt road outside their farm. They rescued him and brought him to the barn. But he got lonely, so they had to find him a friend . . . and it just grew from there.

Nea's story was a bit more creative—there were witches and unicorns and evil magicians who wanted to steal the animals and turn them into evil henchmen. Horace had a feeling Nea and Jones would get along.

"Maybe your father can get the truth out of you." Clary sighed.

Linn shook her head. "You can't tell Poppa. He'll never let us help on the farm again."

"We only took the animals to show him we're good at taking care of them," Nea added.

Eleanor glanced around. "How did you find them all?"

"Mostly we just found them in the neighborhood," Lin said.

Nea nodded. "Except for Mario." She pointed at Princess Sofaneesba. "We got that one on account of Dr. Schwank. He showed us his picture to cheer us up when old Trav got real sick. So we went and got him."

Bunwinkle leaned over to Horace and whispered, "I knew those creepy vets had to be involved somehow."

"And we missed old Trav, so we tried to take

Ms. Higgins's gray horse, but he was too hard to get. So we took the goat." Linn patted Mal on the head.

A gleam came into Mal's eye, and he reared back. If Eleanor hadn't wrestled him down, Horace had no doubt, Linn would've had an enormous lump on her head.

Nea continued the story. "We really did find Blue Sparkles on the road around the bend. That part was true."

When he heard his name, Blue ran to stand by the twins.

Clary stared at him. "Why did you put all that stuff on them?"

"Well, once we got a bunch of animals together, we started thinking it would be fun to open a special petting zoo, but then they needed to be more special." Linn said it as if it should've been obvious.

Eleanor patted her friend on the shoulder. "I think I'm going to take my group and head home. But before I go . . ." She knelt down to look Linn and Nea in the eyes. "I want you two to know what you did was wrong. You can't take things, especially animals, from other people. I spent the last few days worried sick. I'm sure the owners of these other animals felt the same way."

The twins looked down and mumbled, "Sorry."

"I know you wanted to show your parents you could be responsible, but you didn't do that. You didn't take care of these animals. You used human products on them and kept them trapped in cages."

The girls clasped hands but said nothing.

"Eleanor, again"—Clary sighed—"I'm so sorry."

"It's not your fault." Eleanor smiled at her

friend. "And the girls can make it up to me by helping out on the Homestead two days a week, so they can learn to take care of animals properly. How does that sound?"

The older woman nodded. "Sounds good to me. Doesn't it, girls?"

"Yes, Mama," they said in unison.

Eleanor patted Clary on the back. "Good luck with all this."

Bunwinkle talked the whole way home. She told Horace about her abduction, Blue Sparkles, a weird dream she'd had about gravy. She didn't stop talking until Eleanor said, "Okay, you two, let's get you cleaned up."

Bunwinkle's ears perked up, and she tapped her front hooves in her happy dance. "Cleaned Up. That's my best game."

Turned out it was Mal's best game as well. He excelled at falling over into the mud and getting chastised by Eleanor. They played it for a long time. Whatever makeup the twins had used was meant to last.

Horace laughed when Bunwinkle and Mal fell

and splashed Eleanor with mud.

"Okay, I think we're done with that game," she said, winding up the hose.

Finally they were clean—well, as clean as they were going to get without nail polish remover and industrial-strength soap. Mal went back to his pen. Minnie greeted him with a friendly headbutt.

Mal blushed. "Och, Minnie, ye missed me."

Horace and Bunwinkle sat in the sun on the porch while she dried off. A breeze picked up, and she shivered. Horace moved closer to keep her warm.

They sat together, watching Eleanor putter around the Homestead for quite a while. Horace's eyes were just starting to feel heavy when Bunwinkle nudged him with her shoulder.

"Thanks for coming to get me." She gave him a big kiss on his peaches. "I love you, Horace."

He cleared his throat. "I love you too."

"Hey, let's do something. How about we check the pond for ducks?" she suggested.

"Actually, I thought we might play a game of Name That Smell. If you wanted to."

Bunwinkle grinned at him. "If you don't mind

getting your butt kicked."

"You can't beat me. I'm older and wiser."

"I go first." She stuck her snout in the air and breathed in. "I smell . . . potatoes."

Horace sniffed. "I smell . . . lipstick." He smirked at Bunwinkle.

"Hah hah." She bumped him with her shoulder. "Go again, but do it right."

Horace inhaled again, and a wonderful aroma filled his sniffer. "I smell garlic and olive oil and . . ."

They looked at each other. "Food!"

Bunwinkle hopped up and raced toward the door. "Come on, Horace," she called over her shoulder.

"I'm coming, Winkie."

But Horace didn't move right away. He looked around at the Homestead, then lifted his sniffer again and took a deep breath. They were all there—the chicks in their coop, the goats and alpacas in their pens, Smith and Jones in the barn, and strongest of all was the scent of Bunwinkle.

Warmth filled his chest, and he smiled. "I smell our family."

From inside the house Winkie yelled, "Horace, get in here! I think Ellie's making couch potatoes!"

A Note from the Author

Thank you so much for reading *Horace & Bunwinkle*. If you're like me, you've fallen in love with Boston Terriers and potbellied pigs. But before you go rushing off to buy one, there are some important things you should know.

First, there's no such thing as Teacup pigs or Pixie pigs or pigs that stay small. All pigs get big, like 100–200 pounds big. Yeah, that's small compared to farm hogs—they weigh about 900 pounds—but it's still big. If you want to adopt a super-awesome pig like Bunwinkle, remember to do research and ask the breeder lots of questions. Or even better, adopt from a piggy rescue.

Second, all dogs and pigs may not get along as well as Horace and Bunwinkle do. Dogs are hunters by nature and pigs get hunted, which means you may have problems if you put them together. Not all dogs are proper and polite Boston Terriers like Horace.

Third, every kind of pet has specific needs, like diet and exercise. Make sure you know what those are before you adopt one.

—PJ

Acknowledgments

First and foremost, I have to thank my spectacular husband, Neil. All that I am today is because of you. And thank you to my boys, Jeff, Zach, and CJ—you make me laugh and inspire me with your weirdness.

Speaking of inspiration, I have to give a shout-out to my wonder pooch, Rosie, the source of most of Horace's and Bunwinkle's silly antics.

Thank you, thank you, thank you to the amazing Kari Sutherland, agent extraordinaire. I'm so glad you're in my corner. Thanks for always building me up and keeping me on track.

A million more thank-yous to Kristin Rens. I love how much you love my silly but sincere characters. Thank you, and the whole team at Balzer & Bray, for taking a chance on us.

And I will always be grateful to Dave Mottram for your illustrations. You truly brought Horace and Bunwinkle to life.

Special thanks to Better Piggies Rescue of Phoenix, Arizona, for letting me hang out with your crew. I learned so much and gained a huge appreciation for what you do.

I am eternally indebted to all the members of Team PJ who've supported me since I began my writing career. Chris Packard and Natalie Sanchez, thank you for reading terrible early drafts and still telling me I could do it. Namina Forna, Nan Marie Swapp, and Liz Dorathy, thank you for always championing me and boosting me up when I was ready to quit. Janet Clark and Wendy Jorgensen, thank you for believing in Horace and Bunwinkle from the beginning. Stephanie Usrey and her fourth grade class, thank you for allowing me to read that early draft to you. There were many times when your faith in the characters sustained me.

Lastly, I wish to express my gratitude to a loving Heavenly Father, who has guided me on every step of this journey.

Turn the page for a sneak peek of the sequel,
Horace & Bunwinkle:
The Case of the Rascally Raccoon

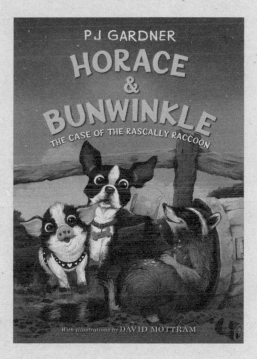

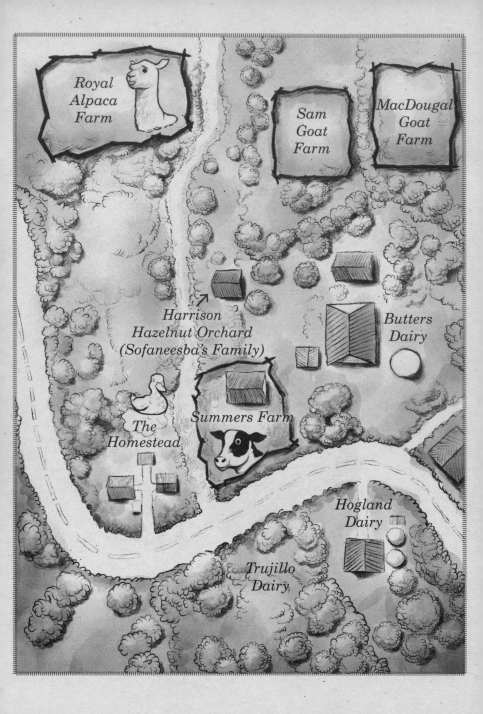

Royal Alpaca Farm

Sam Goat Farm

MacDougal Goat Farm

Harrison Hazelnut Orchard (Sofaneesba's Family)

Butters Dairy

The Homestead

Summers Farm

Hogland Dairy

Trujillo Dairy

1

Garbage, Garbage Everywhere

Winkie was bored silly. Ellie—that was her human—was busy in her office with something called bills, and Horace—that was her brother— was asleep on the couch next to her.

Horace wasn't her blood brother, on account of him being a dog and her being a pig, but they were still family. The kind of family who loved each other no matter what, even when one of them picked a TV show, then immediately fell asleep and didn't even watch. And then his poor sister had to sit through the boringest show ever, about dogs eating toast.

She looked over at Horace, who was drooling on the couch, and made up her mind. The TV was hers. Winkie slowly put a hoof on the remote. There was no movement from the slobber king beside her. Next she pushed the up arrow. A lady's smiling face appeared on the screen and said, "This lipstick will change your life."

Ugh. No, thanks. Lipstick was the worst. Winkie had worn some not long ago, and it took forever to come off.

Winkie pushed the arrow again and a tall man with a furry scarf appeared.

"Welcome to *Weird and Wonderful*. I'm your host, Sheridan Simper, and this little lady is Jojo." The scarf moved, and a pair of beady eyes stared out of the TV. "Jojo is a lemur, and tonight we're going to explore her homeland, Madagascar."

Ooo, this looked good.

Winkie snuggled down to watch, which was the exact moment Horace started to snore. It was kind of a whistle and kind of a snort and it was kind of driving her crazy. Winkie turned up the TV. Horace got louder. She turned it up again and he got louder again. Finally she put her hoof over Horace's nosehole to stop the noise.

Yes! Now she could hear the TV.

She pulled her hoof back and got comfortable.

Sheldon handed Jojo an orange. "Lemurs are big fans of fruit. That's because they're herbivores."

Snore.

Agh, seriously?

"They're also highly intelligent. Using tools and doing simple math are no sweat for these primates."

Sno-o-o-o-o-o-ore.

Winkie did the hoof-on-the-nosehole trick again, but as soon as she covered one nosehole, the other one made the noise. It was like she was playing an instrument.

Dang it! Her show would be over before she could turn off Horace's sniffer.

There was only one thing to do—hooves of steel. It was a move she'd borrowed from a character on her favorite TV show, *Andie's Adventures.* Suey was a pig like Winkie, and she solved mysteries with a dog just like Horace. Only Spot didn't snore or talk about New England constantly.

That was where she and Horace had gotten the idea to be pet-tectives. They were good at it too.

Just last week they'd caught a pair of pet thieves who were rounding up animals from the neighborhood. Mostly because of Winkie, but Horace had helped . . . a little. Things had been quiet since then, but she had a feeling that was about to change.

Horace's nose squeaked again.

That was it! Winkie reared up on her hind legs and shouted, "HOOVES OF STEEL!"

Her feet hit Horace on his side.

"You'll never get me to talk, you disgusting fowl you," he grumbled, but his eyes stayed closed.

No way—he was still asleep! And she'd hit him as hard as she could too. Maybe if she did it again, it would work. Winkie got up on her back legs again and . . .

CLANG!

. . . fell right off the couch.

"What the heck?" Winkie squeaked.

Horace just twitched and mumbled in his sleep. "Ducks. Terrible ducks."

How could he sleep through that?

"Hey, something happened in the courtyard."

4

She nudged him with her snout. "Pet-tectives investigate?"

Horace's noseholes squealed.

"Fine," she said. "I'll go by myself." She clicked her front hooves together. "Pet-*tective*, investigate!"

Winkie didn't understand why Ellie called the space between the house and the barn "the courtyard." That made it sound fancy, but it was really just a gravel driveway. And right now it was a mess.

The trash cans had been knocked over, and the lid to the recycling bin was on the ground next to them. Garbage was everywhere. Empty bottles mixed with used straw from the chicken coop, smeared with Ellie's attempts at cheese making. It was all jumbled together in a big, disgusting wreck.

"Somebody's gonna be in a lot of trouble."

Winkie was almost certain she heard a snort.

"Is someone there?"

Silence.

"Horace?"

She listened extra hard this time. But it was quiet.

Hmm. Maybe she had imagined it.

Then the wind changed direction and an awesome stench filled her snout. There was nothing better than the smell of hot garbage! She grinned. It was Winkie time!

She backed up, then ran, fast as she could, straight into a pile of food scraps. Popcorn, yum!

It was a little soggy, but it still tasted good. Ooo, uncooked pasta—and it was still crunchy! She rooted around and found some grapes and . . . a cloth diaper? Yuck. What was that doing in there?

"You'd better hope Eleanor doesn't catch you

doing that," Horace said in his snootiest voice.

Winkie gasped in surprise, accidentally sucking a grape down her windpipe.

"Agh." She coughed and hacked until her eyes watered. Horace was going to have to do hooves of steel on *her* pretty soon.

Luckily she got the grape out before that happened.

"Good heavens!" Horace patted her on the back. "Are you all right?"

She took a deep breath and nodded, then bent her head to lick up the grape again.

"What are you doing?" he asked suspiciously.

"Getting my food."

Horace kicked it away. "You can't do that. It's covered in drool and dirt."

Winkie chased after the grape. "Tastes good to me."

Horace looked around. "Did you make this mess because you were hungry?"

"I didn't do this."

He hmphed at her.

"No, real—"

"Bunwinkle Irene Higgins! What have you

done?" Ellie's voice came out high-pitched, like a bird's.

Over in the hutch the chicks panicked and screamed, "VULTURE!"

Uh-oh. Winkie was in for it now. Maybe if she looked all sorry and stuff Ellie wouldn't get too mad. Winkie made the saddest face she could and peeked up. But her human wasn't buying it.

"Oh, little pig, I do not have time for any of your antics right now. I've got a job interview at the feed store in fifteen minutes and I can't be late. I *need* this job." Ellie grabbed Winkie and held her at arm's length. "You're going to have to stay in one of the outdoor pens until I get back."

"Aw, not the outdoor pens."

Horace tsked. "Serves you right for knocking over the garbage."

She stuck out her tongue at him. He couldn't see, but it still felt good to do it.

"Hey, Eleanor." An older lady with curly gray hair stood by the gate. "I brought that recipe for ya. Don't know how well it will work with goat cheese, but you're welcome to . . . well, for gosh sakes, would you look at that!"

Horace moved between Ellie and the lady. "Stranger danger!" he barked loudly.

The lady didn't look dangerous to Winkie. She looked like someone's grandma, with big earrings shaped like the letter *B* and a funny T-shirt too. It said ASK ME ABOUT MY KOALIFICATIONS. And the *O*s were koala heads.

"Horace, stop that. This is our friend," Ellie scolded. In a friendlier tone she said, "Sorry, Ms. Butters, I have to take care of something right now."

Okay, that hurt. Winkie was not a something. She was a piglet. And nobody needed to take care of her. They just needed to let *her* take care of the garbage. And by "take care of," she meant eat it.

The butter lady waved her hand. "Stop with that Ms. Butters business. Call me Betty. And let me help. I'll tidy this up while you take care of your animals." She squatted down and started tossing stuff into the trash bin. "Cheese and crackers, your piglet made a heck of a mess."

Winkie turned to glare at the woman . . . and slithered right out of Ellie's hands. She landed, tummy first, on the rocks. For a second she couldn't breathe.

"Oh, little one, I'm so sorry," Ellie bent down and ran a hand over Winkie's head. "Are you okay?"

Horace zoomed to her side. "It's all right. Simply close your eyes and count to ten. It will help you relax."

Count to ten? How was that gonna help her breathe? She needed air, not math.

On top of everything else, Winkie's snout itched like crazy and she couldn't scratch it because she was gonna pass out. She closed her eyes with a whimper.

Out of nowhere a little girl called out, "Pigella Pigerina, are you okay?"

Winkie's eyes snapped open.

Freckles.

Braids.

Overalls.

The Hogland twins!

Winkie's heart started to pound, and she felt dizzy. Suddenly she was caught up in a memory—running in the tall grass behind the barn, small hands gripping her sides, bumping against the ground inside a dark bag. It was like the twins were pignapping her all over again.

"NO!" she squealed. She hopped to her feet and ran before the girls could get her.

"Bunwinkle!" Horace and Ellie called after her.

She would probably get in more trouble now, but it didn't matter. Winkie had to get someplace safe. Someplace she could hide. The barn! There were plenty of places to hide in there.

Fast as a cheetah, Winkie raced inside—and ran snout first into a bale of hay. She fell back on her haunches and blinked her eyes.

Ow, that really hurt. So did her heart. It was beating way too fast.

Something moved beside her, making her squeal again.

11

"Och, yer doin' it wrong. If ye're goin' to haid-butt somethin', ye've got to do it with the *top* of yer noggin.'"

Mal the billy goat stared at her from his pen a few feet away. Winkie shook her head. It was like he wasn't even speaking English.

The sounds of pounding feet and shouting made her scramble up and squirm between a couple bales of hay. Maybe it would be too dark in the barn for them to spot her. Her body shook like Jell-O. She closed her eyes.

"Bunwinkle?" Ellie's voice sounded worried.

"What a cute name for a pig!" Great. The koala lady was there too.

Something tickled Winkie's noseholes. She opened her eyes to see her brother dog's frowning face.

"The twins! Don't let them take me!" Her voice came out high and whiny.

Horace tilted his head, a worried look on his face. "It's all right. No one is going to take you anywhere."

"Pigella, where are you?" one of the girls called out.

Winkie squeaked, "Please, don't let them—"

Mal cut her off with a fierce shout. "Och, ye've come back, ye wee scunners! Ye'll not be taking me again." Then he smashed his head into the gate of his pen.

That's right! The twins *had* petnapped Mal and a bunch of other animals too. But how come he was angry and she was scared?

The twins screamed and jumped back into Betty, who bumped into Ellie, who fell sideways, ramming her shoulder into the shelf next to Smith's stall. Everything—radio, Ellie, and shelf—crashed to the ground.

After that, the barn got really wild. The horses freaked out about their radio, the nanny goats cackled at the chaos, and Winkie shivered like it was January.

What was wrong with her?

An hour later Winkie lay on her piggy bed, snuggled under a blanket, still asking herself the same question. The twins were long gone. They'd hightailed it out of there after Mal had tried to attack. Betty Butters had helped pick up the garbage so

Ellie could get to her interview.

Horace was stretched out next to her, licking his legs. He hadn't said much since everything had happened in the barn, but he would. It was just a matter of time.

"Ah-hem." He cleared his throat.

Winkie tensed up. Here it came—the lecture about misbehaving and keeping a stiff upper lip. Whatever that meant.

Horace turned to look at her. "You appear to be feeling better."

"What?"

"You stopped shaking," he said, "and you're able to focus again."

She turned pink. "Oh yeah. I'm totally focused now. I was out of it earlier 'cause I couldn't breathe."

There was a long pause while Horace stared at her. Time to change the topic.

"Hey," Winkie said, "do you think Ellie is really going to get another job?

He sighed. "She does seem concerned about bills a great deal lately."

It was Winkie's turn to sigh. She'd only asked

the question to distract her brother, but now she was worried.

"And she talks about how much everything costs all the time."

Horace stood tall and said, "Clearly she needs our help." His voice got all snooty, like it always did right before he started talking about New England. "We will find ways to be thrifty and we will be on our best behavior. No more eating food that doesn't belong to us." He gave her a pointed look, then continued. "No more shenanigans. And definitely no more tipping over trash cans."

"I didn't tip anything."

A knock at the door made her jump.